"I'm gonna lay Sawyer said. *"I like being around you, Laurel."*

Her gaze was on the blanket now. "Same here. I'm having a great time. But I meant it when I said that I don't do relationships."

Why don't you? he wanted to ask. But, like her, *he* didn't get in too deep, so he refrained from digging.

"I wasn't blowing smoke about being single and loving it, either," he said.

"So what're you saying? That we should be single together? Friends with benefits?"

A straight shooter, all right. "If it's a bad idea, then just tell me. But I have to say that I don't find many women who aren't aiming for marriage, and it's a relief that you're not."

"Right," she said softly. "Never marriage."

She met his gaze, and it was a liquid blue that made his blood rush through him.

"What if I kissed you," he asked, "just to see how it might work out?"

Dear Reader,

Wow—talk about a wild ride! The Fortunes and their friends have been on a roller coaster of romance and family mysteries these past five books, and things are about to come to a head!

It was such fun to revisit Red Rock, a place I haven't written about since I penned *A Tycoon in Texas* years ago. I'm writing about another sexy rich guy this time—and Sawyer Fortune is such an easygoing flirt that I couldn't help adoring him. Laurel Redmond, a singleton pilot, is more than his match, so enjoy the fireworks!

I hope you visit my website at www.crystal-green.com for contests and up-to-date news. I'm also on Twitter at @CrystalGreenMe. Please drop by and say hi! Mostly, though, I hope you have a sweet, sultry summer—much like the one you're about to read about in Red Rock....

All the best,

Crystal Green

A CHANGE OF FORTUNE

CRYSTAL GREEN

HARLEQUIN® SPECIAL EDITION®

Special thanks and acknowledgment
to Crystal Green for her contribution
to The Fortunes of Texas: Southern Invasion continuity.

Recycling programs
for this product may
not exist in your area.

ISBN-13: 978-0-373-65745-2

A CHANGE OF FORTUNE

Copyright © 2013 by Harlequin Books S.A.

Printed in U.S.A.

Books by Crystal Green

CRYSTAL GREEN

lives near Las Vegas, where she writes for the Harlequin Special Edition and Blaze lines. She loves to read, over-analyze movies and TV programs, practice yoga and travel when she can. You can read more about her at www.crystal-green.com, where she has a blog and contests. Also, you can follow her on Twitter @CrystalGreenMe.

To Marcia Book Adirim, Gail Chasan, Susan Litman
and the hardworking editors and staff
at Harlequin Special Edition,
plus all the authors who worked on this series. Cheers!

Chapter One

Sawyer Fortune had come to the opening of Mendoza's nightclub to have the time of his life.

But if he was honest, every night had pretty much been like that for him from the day he was born.

Money? The Fortunes had more than they knew what to do with.

Opportunity? Right at his fingertips.

Glamour and good times? Check that and that, too.

As he took a seat at the long, old-style cowboy bar under the cursive, neon-pink Wet Your Whistle sign, Sawyer shouldn't have had a care in the world, thanks to his lot in life. Yet somehow he'd ended up with more than a few worries.

Even so, after some beers and conversation with a beautiful woman or two, he expected that all his concerns would fade to the background. That's how it always worked for him. That's how it would work tonight, too.

He took stock of the place: a raised hardwood dance floor crowded with people moving to a loud Kenny Chesney song while its music video played on over-sized screens around the room, neon boot signs lighting the dark corners.

Miguel had done well with this club, reinventing himself, going from being a sales executive at a record company in New York to a nightclub owner here in Red Rock, Texas.

As Sawyer put in his drink order to the bartender, he felt someone slap him on the back. When he turned around, it was Miguel Mendoza himself, beaming in the flush of his club's obvious opening-night success.

"So what do you think?" he asked over the music, his dark eyes glinting. He looked the part of the owner, all right, his black hair trimmed, his midnight shirt and pants a complement to the badass boots that he must've gotten from his wife's company, Castleton Boots.

"What I think," Sawyer said, "is that you're on top of the world. Congratulations. This is really something."

"That's high praise coming from a man who's visited a lot of nightclubs in his day." Miguel took a seat on a rawhide stool next to Sawyer. "This place is more than Red Rock has ever seen, though."

It was the *only* nightclub in Red Rock, Sawyer thought. The town was growing, but it wasn't exactly New York or even Atlanta.

"No club I've ever been to has charm like this," he said. "And charm is hard to come by."

Miguel cocked a brow at Sawyer. "Not for some."

He was talking about all the stories Sawyer had earned with his reputation, which had followed him from Atlanta.

The Fortune playboy. The last of his extended family to have survived the love bug that'd been biting their clan for years now. His *own* branch of the family had been victims of the Plague, as he called it, ever since his sister, Victoria, had succumbed to Garrett Stone, then his brothers had struck out on their own here in Red Rock, finding their own soul mates.

But Sawyer wasn't a carbon copy of his brothers. Sure, like them he'd defected from JMF Financial in Atlanta after a fight with their father, where he was still the de facto director of publicity and marketing, and he'd relocated to Red Rock, too. Yet he was damned if he'd ever get hitched. He also was out to reinvent himself, just as the rest of his family had done since defecting, but he was avoiding the love plague. He'd never met a woman who wasn't so into the Fortunes' money that she wanted him for what he had to offer otherwise.

Ranching and day trading, Sawyer thought, lifting the beer that the bartender had just slid in front of him in a toast to Miguel and his success with the club. This was his new life, and he'd definitely drink to *that* kind of reinvention.

The bartender had brought Miguel a beer, too, and they drank in silence for a moment as the fast song wore away and the DJ wrangled together the folks on the dance floor for a trivia contest and a giveaway featuring Mendoza's T-shirts.

Miguel couldn't stop grinning, watching everything play out. "So this is what it's like to see your dreams come true. Since I was old enough to think about a future, all I wanted to do was open a place like this. It wouldn't mean as much without Nicole, but…"

Sawyer chuckled, and Miguel did, too.

"I know, I know," he said. "You're going to razz me now for becoming one of the love-struck masses."

"Wasn't it just over a year ago at your brother's wedding that we snuck out of that lovey-dovey reception, met each other in the bar where we watched highlights on ESPN from the football games we'd missed that day and you said—"

"That I was never going to get married? Yeah, that was me. You, too. The both of us dyed-in-the-wool bachelors who'd escaped all the wedding silliness, swearing off matrimony."

Sawyer didn't get on Miguel's case too much. After all, Miguel had told Sawyer at that wedding that if he ever did get married, he'd sure as hell invite him to the ceremony, and he'd made good on that promise.

"So," Sawyer said, taking pity on the newlywed because there'd no doubt be a lot of tough times ahead for him. "Where is Nicole?"

"Finishing up some work. You know how it is for those CEO types."

As Miguel smiled, he had no idea of realizing that he'd nicked Sawyer a little with his comment. Sawyer had always known that, as the youngest son of James Marshall Fortune, he didn't have a shot at being a CEO or even a VP. As a matter of fact, he was the only son who didn't hold a high office at JMF Financial, probably because his dad had never trusted his "go with the flow" attitude. It just didn't fit in with the great James Marshall Fortune's steely work ethic.

So what had Sawyer done over the years? Well, he'd been even more easygoing than ever—the opposite of his driven older brothers, that was for sure. He'd become the afterthought that Dad had always expected Sawyer to be, a so-called "reckless" or "careless" man who'd never sought the glory of a corner office.

But that was neither here nor there right now, in a place where he'd left JMF Financial behind—a town where he could wear jeans and boots and Western shirts instead of the suits he'd never been comfortable in.

Still, sitting here, seeing how all Miguel's hard work had paid off sent a pang through Sawyer, as if he should've been more ambitious in life.

"You know I'm not so much of a man with a plan, Miguel." He gestured around the club with his bottle. "I'm not sure I ever had any long-term goals like this... or any, in general."

"What're you talking about? You're a Fortune—you were born with goals."

Sawyer laughed. "Fortune, schmortune. People put too much stock in the name, no pun intended. If you ask me, I'd rather we all change it to Smith and be done."

The name had never meant much to him, even though he loved his family more than anything. It was just that being a Fortune had caused its share of problems, with a lot of women who sought things that came with the name, with expectations that Sawyer didn't want any part of. Hell, it'd almost happened with his brother Shane recently, when they'd suspected that his fiancée, Lia, was a gold digger. Sawyer hadn't been so easygoing *then*.

Truthfully, he'd put her at a wary distance, although he'd tried to make it up to her after they'd found out she was on the up-and-up and was truly in love with Shane.

Whatever "love" was.

"As a Fortune," he said to Miguel, "I probably could've indulged in whatever I wanted throughout the years, but if I was born with anything, it was a predestined life. A career path. I was never expected to dream about opening a nightclub or doing what I wanted. I didn't have much choice but to join the family business."

"Having money and a guaranteed job is not exactly a bad thing, my friend."

Miguel was right. And it wasn't that Sawyer was ungrateful for what he'd been born with, it was just that...

Well, what did it mean to be a Fortune, exactly?

He wasn't sure, had never been sure, and as the years passed, the picture never became any clearer.

Miguel dangled his bottle between his fingers. "What would you do if you could start over from scratch, then? If the mighty Fortunes could buy that kind of do-over?"

Sawyer was surprised his family hadn't found a way to accomplish that very thing, what with their track record of success—something he'd never felt much a part of deep inside, where no one could see what he was really feeling.

He turned Miguel's question over in his mind. Turned it over again. And he'd be damned if he could come up with an answer.

Finally, he said, "You know—if I ever pursued that idea seriously, I don't have the foggiest idea what I'd do."

It came off as a joke—people were used to Sawyer joking—and Miguel laughed once more.

Sawyer played off the moment. He guessed it was sort of funny—a twenty-seven-year-old Fortune as aimless and dissatisfied as he was.

"At any rate," he said, "I'm young and I've got plenty of time to figure everything out."

Miguel, who was about the same age, nodded, and they toasted to that, too.

But this time, Sawyer put his bottle on the bar instead of drinking. Hadn't he already started a do-over by leaving JMF behind and coming out here, setting down stakes on New Fortunes Ranch and going in a different life direction?

Yet did that matter when the biggest reason he'd left Atlanta behind was because he and his siblings had suffered a falling-out with Dad?

So many secrets… That was what had pushed Sawyer and his brothers, Shane, Asher and Wyatt, from JMF in the first place. They'd found out that their father had left half his shares in the business to a mysterious woman named Jeanne Marie and, at first, they'd suspected that he was a bigamist. There'd been a major blowup with Dad about that. But why *shouldn't* their minds be reeling with suspicion when her last name had been Fortune, too? And just why would Dad have left all those assets to her?

Then, after they'd made the decision to distance themselves from their father and JMF Financial…*then* they'd met Jeanne Marie and discovered that she was actually Dad's twin sister, and it'd thrown the family into a real tizzy. More questions had blown around them: Why hadn't Dad just told them the truth? And why hadn't he come to Red Rock yet to come clean with all of them?

James was scheduled to arrive next week to finally explain everything. Sawyer, more than anyone else, had been trying to keep an open mind about his intentions, which was ironic, considering Sawyer had always felt like Dad's least favorite.

The youngest, the afterthought. The son least like the grand tycoon.

But maybe that's exactly why Sawyer was slow to hop on the doubt-ridden bandwagon—because this was the one time he could matter to Dad.

And maybe not.

As Miguel chatted briefly with the bartender, Sawyer's gaze skimmed the club again. A band was setting up on a stage and the DJ was ending the giveaway by whipping the crowd into a hooting rise of enthusiasm for the last prize—a hundred-dollar gift certificate to Red, the most popular restaurant in town.

But Sawyer didn't dwell on the entertainment too much—he hadn't come here for the band or the DJ. Miguel had done quite a job getting women into his club—gorgeous ones, too. Texas belles with tiny waists, tight T-shirts, short skirts and fancy boots.

When his gaze came back to the bar, traveling over the women sitting on stools, it stopped on one in particular.

And…damn. She was willowy, with long, straight blond hair that streamed down her back. From where he was sitting, he could tell that she wasn't gussied up for a night out. It was the opposite, actually, because she was dressed in a plain white T-shirt that clung to her curves, plus faded jeans that had been worn in just enough to shape a perfect derriere. When he saw her red boots, it was a bit of a surprise, seeing as he'd taken her for the type who was trying not to stand out, despite her good looks.

Was she waiting for someone while she leaned her elbows on the bar and nursed a bottle of soda?

Miguel had stopped talking with the bartender.

"You might want to think twice about that one," he said.

"Why?" For the first time tonight, Sawyer had been in a much better mood, just from looking at her. "Weren't we talking about having some goals? She seems like a pretty good one for now."

"You dive-bomb her with that attitude and you're going to get shot down. Laurel Redmond isn't what you'd call an easy pickup, Sawyer."

Not easy, huh? Maybe he was tired of easy. Something different sounded just fine to him, seeing as he'd gotten tired of the gold diggers, gotten tired of always being so instinctively cautious with all the "easy" women.

Miguel added, "I have no idea why she even came here. From what I know, she's not exactly a barfly or... Well, just watch. You'll see."

A cowboy had sauntered up to the bar, cozying right next to Laurel Redmond. She didn't even glance over at him. Uh-uh. She just sat there, cool and reserved, even as he pushed back the brim of his hat to blatantly check her out.

"Keep watching," Miguel said, clearly entertained.

When the cowboy leaned over to say something, all she did was utter one short sentence. He drew back from her and was gone in a flash.

"*That's* what I've heard about Laurel Redmond,"

Miguel said. "I don't know the woman myself—she's been in Red Rock for nearly a year, I think, and I've mostly been in New York—but she's got a reputation as big as yours."

"She's the girl about town?"

"The opposite. She's as independent as they come. Enjoys her own company. Ambitious as hell. They say she's got a real chip on her shoulder from her time as a pilot in the Air Force—she always wanted to prove herself as a woman there and rise above the standards they set. Cream of the crop, you know?"

"In short, she's not just a pretty face."

"Yeah, but I wouldn't ever mention those last two words to her. My God, she might throw you across the room."

Sawyer took another gander. Even if *he* wasn't the most ambitious man around, a challenge sounded like just the thing.

"She doesn't look like that much of a bully," he said.

When another man—a silk-shirt-wearing, hair-slicked-back guy—approached her, all she did was mutter one sentence to him again, and he was off and away.

What was she saying that was so effective?

Sawyer couldn't help himself. He took his beer in hand, hooking a thumb in the belt loop of his jeans. "Don't mind if I do, Miguel. Thanks for the warnings, though."

Miguel shook his head. "It's your ego. But one last thing to remember—she's Tanner Redmond's little sister."

Sawyer definitely knew Tanner—he was married to

Sawyer's cousin Jordana and was an ex-Air Force pilot, just like his little sis.

It hit Sawyer then. He'd actually seen Laurel at Jordana's wedding, but she'd had her hair pulled into an upswept style that made her look more polished than she did tonight, and she'd seemed uncomfortable in her fancy dress. She'd also stayed far from the dance floor, and she might've even left early. Sawyer had been pretty distracted that night, so he wasn't sure.

Tonight, though, she was relaxed, obviously not out to impress anyone, and Sawyer couldn't take his eyes off her.

Miguel sighed. "If you know Tanner, then you realize he's going to be on your case if you—"

"I'm not out to make trouble with her." Family was everything to Sawyer. Even when James had told his sons that he felt betrayed by their defection, Sawyer had still felt a certain loyalty, defending him during the whole Jeanne Marie scandal.

Why? Well, he'd just have to see if Dad had been worth the effort when he got to Red Rock.

He brushed off his worries and shook Miguel's hand, congratulating him again.

But down the bar, another man was already making his move on Laurel.

"Good luck," Miguel said, staying on his stool at the bar.

A front-row seat?

Great. But Sawyer wasn't planning on crashing and burning, as Miguel had predicted he would.

When it came to meeting women, Sawyer Fortune always flew pretty high.

* * *

Laurel could feel yet another guy sidling up to her, eyeing her.

This again.

She didn't look at him as she said, "Not to be rude, but I'm not on the meat market, understand?"

The brush-off was milder than most, but just as to-the-point as always. Thank God the guy split. Good thing, too, because she wasn't into preppy stuff like red-and-black checkered shirts and khakis—two elements of his wardrobe she'd seen from her peripheral vision.

Honestly, she wasn't into cowboy hats or disco duds or…heck, just about everything she'd seen in this club tonight.

She'd had a long day at work, flying a businessman connected with one of the Fortune companies to Houston, then Dallas, then back here. But that's what she did for a living now—charter flights, flying lessons—and she usually loved it.

Except when the client made what he thought were funny, subtle innuendos the entire day about her landing the plane and stopping at a hotel with him.

She'd held her tongue, but when she'd come back from the airport to the Redmond's Flight School office, she'd told Tanner to strike this client from their customer list. No jerks allowed.

She was still the new girl at work, but she had no problem speaking up.

As she sipped her soda, she mellowed. She'd only come out here tonight to see what the fuss was about, not to find out how many guys she could shoot down. And maybe, just maybe, she'd wanted to get out of her apartment since it was the beginning of summer, and she'd always loved summers in the south with their long days and lazy sounds. And when you compared the heat to some of the places she'd been the past years, where the desert fried you through to the bone, summers here were to be treasured.

She looked up and watched the TV, which was playing a soccer match, totally drowned out by the start of a Tim McGraw song.

And that's when she felt another guy coming in for a flyby.

Maybe her back wouldn't have stiffened if she hadn't spent her entire life fighting off the advances of men who thought she was just nice to look at and that's it. Maybe it had something to do with a dad who'd taught her early and well that guys didn't stay. Or maybe she was remembering how that lesson had been emphasized during the one and only time she'd fallen in love, only to be robbed of her heart as well as her bank account.

Her tongue itched to say something preemptive to this pickup artist, too, but as she felt him coming close to her, she smelled leather—an expensive kind of scent— and she wasn't sure if it was from a fancy saddle or an office chair.

Something about the scent of him piqued her curiosity, and she slyly glanced over.

As an unidentified feeling violently jumped in her chest, she almost looked away before he could read the sudden attraction on her face.

Almost. Because, damn, he had the bluest eyes. And thick, dark, sand-brown hair. Tall. Solid with muscle, dressed in his jeans and an untucked white Western shirt with faint embroidery.

The capper was a smile that melted the iceberg in her—just the tip, but there *was* a heat that she couldn't deny, tossing and turning in her. It was the sexy smile that told her this one was too confident to be chased off.

"You look bored," he said in a voice that reminded her of thick, rich cream. "You should be out there dancing."

She was a creature of habit, and no matter how hot he was, her defenses were already up. "I don't dance."

He didn't seem taken aback. It was actually the opposite—the guy was amused.

"We're in a dance club," he said over the music. "I don't think it's out of line to ask you to dance, especially when you've been tapping your boot since this song started."

She hadn't realized it, but he was right, and she stopped tapping, pronto.

But she felt like starting up again, out of a jumpy sort of adrenaline rush this time, because those baby blues were locking with her gaze so...

Um, hotly?

She blinked, then made sure she was still in the leave-me-to-my-drink posture she'd adapted since sitting down.

"Dancing's really not my thing," she said, hoping that would do it.

He laughed, low and nice. Nice for flipping her traitor belly upside down, that is.

"You don't remember me, do you?" he asked.

She allowed herself to take a long look at him—even

longer than she had before—and then shook her head. "Afraid I don't."

"We're almost family."

She kept shaking her head.

"Then here's a hint," he said. "Your brother's wedding last year…?"

"Nope." She hadn't exactly been in a social mood at the wedding—imagine that—and she'd kept to herself most of the time. Even years after her breakup she'd still been smarting, especially at an event that was so full of hearts and flowers, which she didn't believe in anymore. She'd been overjoyed for Tanner, but being totally dumped and worked over by Mr. Crappy Boyfriend had soured her on love for the rest of her life, and she'd just wanted to curl into a ball in her room, not facing anyone. She'd wanted to tell Tanner that even if he was happy now, it wouldn't work out. Didn't he remember what'd happened to Mom when their father had left?

No one needed That Girl at a wedding, so she'd gone home early. But she'd been wrong about Tanner's marriage—he and Jordana were as happy as could be, with a baby who was as sweet as apple pie.

She smiled to herself, thinking of little Jack, and the hot man in front of her picked up on her improved disposition.

"You may not remember me," he said, "but I remember spotting you at the wedding."

"Sorry about that." She took a sip of her drink.

Was he going to go away? Finally leave her in peace?

Fat chance. He'd set his beer on the bar, as if he'd claimed the area next to her.

And why did part of her not mind?

She sneaked another glance at him, and her heart tumbled. Yeah, *her* heart, doing gymnastics like it was on a balance beam, not quite falling off, but not quite stable, either.

But it felt…refreshing. She hadn't experienced a reaction like this in such a long time. What if…?

Oh, no. No what-ifs. They'd gotten her into trouble with Steve Lucas, when she'd given him all her trust, all her emotions.

And access to her bank account.

The fast song that'd been playing melded into a slow one. Vintage Willie Nelson. Romantic, lazy—just like the summer days she'd always loved.

Hot Wedding Guy must've seen her loosen up, even just for a moment, because he bent a bit closer, warming her ear with his words.

"Last chance to dance."

Who was he, and what was he doing to her?

She sent a lowered look his way. "You're going to be on me all night about this, aren't you?"

"Probably. But if you want me to bug off, all you have to do is say so."

She thought of a hundred excuses to chase him away: she had a boyfriend. (Ha!) She had to get home to wash her hair. (Clean as a whistle.)

But…those blue eyes. That smile.

My God.

"See?" he said, all lethal charm. "You do want to dance."

"How do you know?"

"Because you would've already zapped me, just like

you've been doing to every other guy who dared to break through your force field."

"How—?"

"I couldn't help seeing you in action." He jerked his chin toward a spot down the bar, where he'd probably been sitting.

He did it in such an assured, masculine way that another spike of attraction bolted through her, making her shift in her seat.

She melted a little more. Dammit. But she didn't look where he'd gestured.

"Why were you at that wedding?" she asked instead.

"Jordana's my cousin."

He was a Fortune? And he seemed very pleased that she hadn't noticed that fact right away.

How often did he go undetected by someone when the family was always in the papers? Had he been enjoying that she hadn't known him from Adam just now?

The slow song was in full play, couples two-stepping around the dance floor.

Still, he stood there, smiling that smile, breaking her down second by second.

Okay. Would one dance do any harm? After all, it *was* fun to be flirting. She'd almost forgotten how liberating it was. Just because she was doing it didn't mean they'd have to get engaged or anything.

"All right," she said. "One song."

He angled his head in acknowledgment. Teasingly? Whatever it was, she couldn't help but bite back her own smile.

Flirting. Just a little. Just for a short time, then she'd go home.

She left her drink at the bar, and Blue Eyes did the same with his beer. The bartender nodded at them, silently promising he'd save her place.

Then, on the floor, the guy took her in his arms, and it felt…

Good God, it felt better than she'd remembered.

Being held, feeling a man's strong arms around her, allowing him to guide her.

Hormones skittered through her, and she gave way to them. Why not? What was the harm for five damn minutes?

"Which cousin did you say you were?" she asked as they began to circle the floor.

"Jordana's."

"Stop teasing. I'm asking your name."

He seemed to recognize that she'd given up a smidge of ground, and he grinned at her, twirling her stomach once again.

She held back another smile. Oh, but he was cute.

"I'm Sawyer," he said.

As in Tom, she thought. Playful, clever Tom Sawyer, and now that she heard his name, she realized that she'd gotten wind of this man before, through reputation only. Her brother had warned her about his tomcat ways prior to the wedding, when Tanner had given her the rundown about their new in-laws.

But this wouldn't go far enough to merit caution, she thought as Sawyer led her, firmly yet smoothly, in a dance he'd obviously danced many times before with other women.

Even so, when he swooped her into an unexpected

spin and smiled that gorgeous smile down at her, her stomach twirled once again.

"See," he said, "I knew you wouldn't be able to resist."

And, indeed, she couldn't.

Chapter Two

The dancing had only just begun for Sawyer.

As he lifted Laurel Redmond back up and continued with the two-stepping, her blond hair brushed his chin. She was tall enough that he could smell the shampoo she used and the soap on her skin—something clean but not flowery. Something just right for a woman whose hand felt the tiniest bit rough from the work she did as a pilot.

Just right for a woman who had been keeping him guessing for the past fifteen minutes.

He led her around the floor, both of them not talking, just flowing to the music. He liked the way she moved. Liked that they were getting looks from others in the room, as if they'd been dancing together for a while.

Most of all, though, he liked that she'd clearly been interested in him *before* he'd told her that he was a Fortune.

He'd been able to see that she was drawn to him by the flush on her cheeks and the way she'd sassed him at the bar. Maybe she was a tough talker, but there was also a softness to her, another dimension to her that he wasn't sure she liked to flaunt.

When the song ended, he didn't let her go. At first, she didn't make a move to release herself from him, either.

They just looked at each other.

Bluebonnet eyes, he thought, remembering the spring flowers he'd seen during rides across the property of the New Fortunes Ranch.

A second passed. Two. Heartbeats climbing on top of each other in his chest.

But when the DJ started yammering about another giveaway, Laurel pulled back from him. He could've sworn that she looked a bit disappointed—at the lack of music? That their dance was over?—as she headed for the few steps that raised the dance floor from ground level.

He wasn't far behind her. No way was he letting her run off.

"I hear you're pretty new in town," he said over the DJ's voice.

"I've been here since last summer," she responded over her shoulder.

"That's new enough."

"*You're* new. At least relatively. I know because I read the papers."

"How about I buy you a drink to mark our entry into Red Rock society?"

She didn't answer until they wound through the crowd and got to the bar, where she snagged her drink from between two cowgirls who'd bellied up to her place and closed ranks over it, all but taking over her stool.

"No booze for me, thanks," she finally said to him when she had her beverage in hand. She lifted it. "I'm sticking to soda tonight."

Whether she realized it or not, she was having a conversation with him. _From a shut-down to this,_ he thought. Not too bad.

"But you usually do drink?" he asked.

A Garth Brooks song started playing, and he had to bend closer to hear her.

"I'm flying tomorrow," she said in his ear. "I never indulge the night before."

The warmth of her breath against his cheek sent a whir spinning through him, like propellers ready to go.

He took a chance, inching even closer to her.

And miracle of miracles, she didn't flinch away.

"Is it a charter flight or a lesson?" he asked.

She pulled back to give him a raised eyebrow. "Lessons. Hey, you do your homework on a girl, don't you?"

"When it's worth my time."

The eyebrow stayed raised. A few beats of music passed, and he wondered if she'd come to a crossroads with him.

Was she about to tell him to get lost now that she'd given him his dance?

When she began moseying toward the back of the club, where a neon arrow pointed down over a sign that said Play Time, he lifted his own brow.

He grabbed his beer from the bar and went where she led. She still had him guessing, and it was working like a charm.

She glanced over her shoulder, just as if she'd expected him to follow her like a lovelorn pup.

A point to the lady.

When they got to the Play Time room, it was a breath of fresher, quieter air. The spot wasn't populated yet—only with pool tables and dartboards and skee ball, plus old-model video games.

"So do you ever take a day off?" he asked, continuing the discussion as if it'd never stopped.

"About once a week." She inspected a vintage *Space Invaders* game, then smiled, almost as if to herself. "Sometimes not at all."

Something had definitely changed with her from first contact to now, and it was confusing the tar out of him. Miguel had said she was fiercely independent and not one to be messed with, but it was becoming clear that Laurel Redmond was mainly confident and self-assured. Just because she'd wanted some privacy at the bar didn't make her antisocial.

Especially now, as she gave him a long look, then moved away from *Space Invaders*.

That look fired Sawyer up, scratching heat against the lining of his belly.

As she wandered off to a *Galaga* game, he watched how she moved—easily, comfortable in her lean body, holding her drink in one hand, dragging the other over the joystick on the console.

He got his mind off joysticks for his own good.

"You seem young to be so accomplished," he said. "A pilot in the Air Force, now a civilian flyer."

"Again, you studied up." She sipped from her soda, her throat working as she swallowed, thoroughly surveying *him* now.

Was she flirting with him as hard as he'd been flirting with her? Giving as good as she'd gotten after a warm-up period?

She leaned back against the video game. "Long story short, I was in the military, I got out, then Tanner got married. Jordana was also pregnant, and I wanted to be around to see their baby grow up."

"Jack," he said, thinking of the nearly nine-month-old child. "I've met him. Cute little bugger."

When a sweet smile lit over her mouth, he knew he'd hit a button in her. But she turned away from him before he could keep talking about her baby nephew.

"Anyway," she said, as she sauntered by the wall of skee-ball lanes, "I suppose you're right. I've done more than most people at this point in life."

He wouldn't ask how old she was—women generally didn't take too kindly to that—but he guessed she was around his age.

"You must've gone in the military right out of high school," he said.

"No, but I knew what I wanted and applied myself so I could join right after I graduated from college." She shrugged, as if it was no big deal. "Luckily, I skipped a couple grades in grammar school, then graduated from high school early and made quick work of my university time."

"You never doubted what you wanted to do?"

"Nope. I wanted to be a pilot just like my brother Tanner." Her voice had gotten sort of dreamy. "So I made note of everything he did to get into the AF, and I tried to do it better and faster. I went for a degree in physics in college, joined the ROTC and went to flight school on the weekends, working nights so I could afford the lessons."

"You got a private pilot's license."

"Exactly."

She tilted her head, considering him, her long hair shimmering as the neon from a few games caught it. In her white T-shirt and jeans, she looked like a model for a beer ad, a male fantasy of a "cool girl" and "womanly woman" that rarely existed.

Sawyer was fascinated. And impressed. She really wasn't just another pretty face.

"What do you know about a private pilot's license?" she asked.

"Just that I have one." He wasn't going to tell her about his Gulfstream jet that he'd left in a hangar in Atlanta, just waiting for him to use it. Then again, he had a lot of toys he'd put aside after he'd lost interest in his old life.

A woman who'd stuck to her dreams and did everything in her power to make them come true wouldn't be impressed.

And rightly so.

But he didn't dwell on his shortcomings. He never did. It was the only way he'd survived years of his father's expectations.

Laurel was watching him closely again, as if she was assessing him, like she was doing to each video game she passed.

Time to put the attention elsewhere so she wouldn't look too hard.

"You must've done a lot of traveling in the Air Force," he said. "Do you miss it?"

She meandered over to one of those old-fashioned fortune-tellers in a box, where the name Madame Luna was painted on the glass just above the black-haired, green-scarf-clad gypsy mannequin holding a crystal ball.

"I do," Laurel said. "You know, I got out of the reserves pretty recently, so it's weird to hear you refer to my time in the AF in the past tense. It's been a part of me for so long, even when I was just aiming to join up."

"Where did you travel?"

Her face darkened. "Listen, if I told you about my missions, I'd have to kill you."

But when she slid him an impish smile, he realized she was toying with him.

A sense of humor, smart, driven, capable... He felt like a huge slacker next to her. The most trouble he'd ever had to face was in the Fortune boardroom.

She was reaching into her front jeans pocket, pulling out some change.

"Get over here," she said. "We've talked enough about the past. It's time for the future. Yours first."

He kind of liked being ordered around by a sexy airman. "Right away."

She smiled, then put the money into the fortune-teller's coin slot. After Sawyer ambled over, he took one more drink of his beer, then set it down where she'd put her beverage, on a nearby table.

Madame Luna started to wave her stiff hand over her crystal ball. Not long afterward, a slip of paper rolled out of the contraption, and she went still again.

Laurel read his fortune to herself, her face stoic.

"Should I prepare for a good future or bad?" Sawyer asked.

With a suspicious look—as if he'd sneaked in here and planted the paper beforehand—she gave it to him.

"'You will meet a tall, dark, handsome stranger,'" he read, smiling at her, giving the slip back. "I think that's *yours*, not mine, and it looks like it already came true."

"Well, at least you're tall," she said.

Zing. She'd gotten him.

She was smiling a little, obviously at her joke, as she crumbled up the paper in her hand and peered at the fortune-teller. "Madame Luna should know that I'm not in the market for any cheap lines, anyway."

She followed up with a glance to Sawyer that clearly said, *And for your information, just because I'm hanging around with you right now, that doesn't mean I'm up for an easy hookup, either.*

Message received.

This time he put money into the machine, and Madame Luna came up with *his* future.

"'Your lucky number,'" he read, "'is thirteen.'"

"Lucky number!" Laurel started laughing, tickled by the comment.

"What's so funny about that?"

"Because," she said, already wandering away from him, "I had your number right away, Fortune. You didn't need Madame Luna to give one to you."

He chuckled. "You think you know me that well."

She turned around, walking backward, as if she had eyes in the rear of her head. Come to think of it, from the way she'd barely looked at all the men who'd approached her earlier before shooting them down, she probably did.

"Let me see," she said in a voice a fortune-teller might use. "The man I see before me has never had to work for anything his entire life. Yes?"

Another zing.

"And," she continued, "it all comes so easily for you."

Another zing.

"Okay, I get it," he said. "You've had to work ten times as hard as I ever did to get what you want. In comparison, my life is a cakewalk. Anything else?"

She stopped, just before her back made contact with a *Pac-Man* game. Her voice sobered. "I wouldn't exactly say it's a cakewalk. I know you've had a rough time lately and I shouldn't give you hell about anything. I've heard about your latest family drama. There's gossip all over the place about how you've suddenly found a long-lost aunt. It's all anyone in Red Rock can talk about these days."

"So it is."

"But you don't seem overly upset about it."

Sawyer shrugged. She'd no doubt gotten straight As in science and every other subject she'd attempted, but he'd always aced the courses in how to hide what he really felt.

"To tell you the truth, I'm not upset. I think it's pretty great that there're more Fortunes out there."

And now that he'd said it, he knew he actually meant it. When he'd first met Jeanne Marie, he'd been as suspicious about her motives as he would be with anyone who stood to gain from those majority JMF shares James had given to her. But Sawyer had quickly warmed up to her after learning that she was his father's twin.

It was his father he was having some issues with.

Laurel was smiling at his answer, but then she got thoughtful. "I can't imagine what it'd be like to have a big family. For as long as I can recall, it's just been me, my two brothers and Mom. No aunts or uncles, cousins or grandparents."

For the first time, he felt sorry for this overachiever. But then she said something that made him nearly balk.

"Someday, *I'd* like to have a really big family."

The words knocked against him. And here he'd thought she was different. Didn't every woman he'd ever met want kids and a mansion to go with them?

Game over. Sawyer didn't want to get involved with a woman whose biological clock was ticking and whose inner calculator was clacking.

She was laughing, and she was doing it hard, holding her belly. When she spoke, she could barely get the words out.

"You…should see…your face…"

What?

After he paused and took stock of the überfrown he'd been wearing, he laughed, too.

He just wished he knew if she'd been truly joking about having a big family or not.

When their mirth faded, Laurel leaned against the *Pac-Man* machine. The considering look she gave him was different. Not assessing, exactly. It was as if he'd passed some kind of test for her.

The thing was, he had no idea what subject they were on right now. Come Home With Me Tonight 101? Introduction to My Bed?

No way. Not after she'd dropped that bomb about populating the world with her kids—a goal that definitely was not in a confirmed bachelor's future.

"Did you think I was sizing you up for daddy material or something?" she asked. "Is that why you suddenly looked like you wanted to sprint out of here?"

"It crossed my mind."

"Women probably have those thoughts about you all the time, right, Fortune? You're probably the most eligible bachelor in the South."

Were they about to transition into "What can you give me, Sawyer Fortune? I can give you whatever you want tonight if you'll give me what I ask for..."

But Laurel just rolled her eyes. "Believe me, when I have kids, it'll be on my *own* terms."

"What do you mean?"

"Adoption. A sperm bank. I don't see myself ever getting married, and I know I'd be a good single parent. A happy one."

He didn't know what to say. Was she for real?

She added, "Don't look so shocked. I love being single. I've got *no* interest in catching the Red Rock wedding bug. Ever."

Word by word, her meaning saturated him. She could've been his mental twin.

"You mean the Plague," he said. "That's what I've been calling it. It's like there's something in the water in this town."

"Or there's some kind of nefarious social experiment going on that no one can figure out. Except for us, of course."

She walked back to Madame Luna's box, fetching

their drinks, giving his beer to him and toasting him with her beverage.

"So about the Red Rock Plague..." she said. "Promise that you'll put me out of my misery if it gets me, okay?"

"Ditto."

He drank to that, thinking that this just might be the start of a beautiful friendship.

Early the next morning, after Sawyer had doused himself under one of the rain showers he'd had installed in his two-story adobe-style ranch house, he went downstairs to find his older brother, Shane, at the small table in the breakfast nook.

He was going over the plans for his own house, which was being constructed. Meanwhile, he was Sawyer's houseguest, along with his pregnant fiancée, Lia, who was no doubt still sleeping.

Sawyer went to the coffeemaker, pouring himself a strong, black cup. Carmen, the cook, must've put it on at the crack of dawn.

"What's the grin about?" Shane asked.

"I had an interesting night."

"At Mendoza's. Yeah, you single guys have all the fun."

But Shane's smile told Sawyer that he hadn't missed the grand opening at all. He'd probably been snuggling with Lia the whole time.

"So," Shane said, sliding the house plans aside. "Can I expect to run into your interesting night as she sneaks out of the house this morning?"

"Very funny. What I meant is that I met a woman who's...different."

Shane perked up at that. "Now there's a description. *Different*. It gives me hope for you yet."

"Don't get excited—I haven't caught the love bug. I'm immune."

"That's what we all said."

"But I'll never stop saying it." He thought of Laurel's matching philosophy. "I met someone who's a lot like me—a person who isn't into marriage. Someone who enjoys her freedom. And when I left Mendoza's last night, she gave me her number. I told her that I wanted to brush up on my flying lessons and—"

"Okay, first off, is that what you're calling it nowadays? Flying lessons? Second, it sounds like she isn't that different from all the other women you've *flown* with over the years. Third, there's only one woman who gives actual flying lessons in the area."

"Right. Laurel Redmond."

Shane leaned back in his chair, letting out a low whistle.

"Say it," Sawyer muttered.

"I remember her from Jordana's wedding, but I've heard about her since. She *is* different, not your type at all."

Very much my type, Sawyer thought. The same bachelor/bachelorette brain, the same allergies to having strings attached.

"She doesn't want anything serious," Sawyer said. "That's why we got along so well last night."

"Well, best of luck to her. She has no idea what's about to hit."

He went back to his house plans, and Sawyer ignored Shane's pessimism as he went about putting together a plate from the small buffet of eggs, croissants and fruit Carmen had set out. By the time he sat at the table, Shane had knocked off the brotherly ribbing altogether.

"I've got some news about Dad," he said.

Sawyer felt the worry coming back full force. So much for last night's fun and games blocking it all out.

"What is it?" he asked.

"I found out that he's been on an overseas trip with Mom. She called Victoria last night, totally unaware that we didn't know where they'd gone. She said she left an itinerary with Dad's assistant."

"He probably instructed her not to give it to us. You know how he's been keeping us in the dark about everything."

"I think you're right. And there we were, taking such pains to see that Mom didn't have a clue about Jeanne Marie. But it turns out she knows everything."

"Huh. Well, maybe Dad told Mom not to say a word to us until he has all his ducks in a row, knowing how upset we've been with him."

"That's what Mom told Victoria." Shane gave Sawyer an appreciative glance. "You've kept your cool about this way more than anyone else, though."

"Dad still has a lot of explaining to do next week, so I'm waiting to see if he's as forthcoming as he needs to be. I wonder if he's told Mom about giving Jeanne Marie half of the JMF Financial majority shares."

"He did."

"And *that* doesn't bother her?"

"Victoria said that Mom's very Zen about all this, but we'll be able to see her true reaction when she gets here with Dad next Monday."

Monday. Sawyer had a birthday just before that, but he wasn't surprised his father had scheduled a trip out of the country at that time. He knew Mom would make up for it, though. She always sent birthday gifts to him during his travels.

The hum of the refrigerator and the tick of the clock over the sink marked the seconds until Shane spoke in a tight voice.

"I swear, Sawyer. I'm not sure I'll ever forgive Dad for what he's done to this family. Wyatt and Asher are still fuming, too. They don't even want him at our triple wedding."

"Dad wouldn't dare miss three of his sons getting hitched, much less one. He'll somehow get into your good graces."

Sawyer tried not to sound bitter about that. James Marshall Fortune had his favorites.

"Whatever Dad does," Shane said, getting out of his seat, "I'm fully expecting you to make it a quadruple wedding, Sawyer. You just wait and see."

With the mood lightened, they both laughed at the very idea of Sawyer getting married.

Didn't everybody?

Laurel was in the flight school office, which had been remodeled after the tornado that'd hit Red Rock last year.

It was bright and early, perfect for going over paperwork. But it was hard to concentrate on all that when thoughts of Sawyer Fortune kept intruding.

Those blue eyes, that smile…and, much to her shock, she'd had a great time with him last night. So great that, when he'd mentioned taking flying lessons, she'd told him to contact her.

It'd been an impulsive response, to be sure, and that was something Laurel certainly was not. Impulsive. She normally planned *everything.* She had backup plans, and even backup plans to her backup plans.

Mostly because things didn't come as easily to her as they had to Sawyer.

The man I see before me has never had to work for anything his entire life, she'd told him. And from the look on his face, she'd hit a target. She'd been kidding around mainly, but she'd halfway meant it, too.

She worked damned hard for what she had, mostly because her mother had taught her that she shouldn't rely on looks. So she'd fought for everything, and it'd only gotten harder in the Air Force, where she'd felt she had to be twice as good as her male counterparts to get ahead....

Her cell phone rang, and she glanced at the ID screen. An unfamiliar number. So she answered professionally.

"Laurel Redmond speaking."

"Just the woman I'm looking for," said a low, drawling voice that spun her sideways and back.

She paused, not because she didn't remember the voice—how could she forget it?—but because she was catching her breath.

Sawyer.

"Laurel? You there?"

"I'm here. You were serious about those lessons, huh?"

"Funny, there aren't many people who'd say I'm serious about much, Laur."

She wanted to correct him. *It's Laurel*. But she liked the Georgia-inflected way he said it, drawing out the one syllable, as if trying to make it last longer than it should.

"When were you thinking of booking the lesson?" she asked, barely aware that she'd leaned her elbows on the desk, like a teenager in a fifties musical.

"I can play around with my schedule. How about you?"

Play around. Nope, she wasn't going to think he'd said it purposely.

"Today and tomorrow are full," she said. "And I'm off work the day after. Then I've got a string of charter flights the rest of the week."

"Off the day after tomorrow, huh? Do you do much riding where you came from?"

"In the Air Force?" It was as much of a home as she'd ever had. "Not really. I haven't ridden a horse in…hell, years."

Not since she was a teenager and she'd volunteered at a ranch for troubled kids who took care of horses as part of their therapy. She'd loved the work, but on a more practical level, it'd also looked great to the college-scholarship committees.

"Years?" he said. "Then I think it's time you got back in the saddle, Laurel Redmond. What do you say you come over on your day off and we postpone those flying lessons for now? I'll have my cook whip something up that you like and we'll ride out to a nice spot where we can laugh about all the poor married people in Red Rock."

Was she really considering this? Hanging out with Sawyer Fortune, flirting a little more with him?

Yes. Yes, she was.

Someone came through the open door to the office, and she glanced up to see her brother with an iPad in hand. He wanted to go over scheduling with her.

She waved him out, but that only made Tanner realize that she was trying to hide something. He leaned against the wall, his dark eyes full of questions as he nodded toward the phone.

She tried to shoo him off again while wrapping up the discussion with Sawyer.

"The day after tomorrow will be great," she said, totally professional once more.

"How about nine o'clock? We'll have brunch, beat the heat by getting out to ride early. You know where New Fortunes Ranch is?"

"I can GPS it."

"Forget that." He gave her directions from the airport.

"Thank you."

If he'd been bewildered by her change in tone, he didn't say it, and they both hung up. Laurel laid her phone on the desk and expectantly looked at Tanner.

"You know," he said, "I could hear you chirping away on the phone before I came in."

Chirping?

"It was business," she said. "As in, none of yours."

Tanner chuckled. "I wasn't sure it was really you. You haven't sounded that lighthearted since…"

He trailed off, but she knew where he'd been going.

"Since Steve, right?" she asked.

"Yeah." Tanner's jaw tightened. "It's been about two years since that lout screwed you over, but it feels like yesterday. I still want to throttle him."

Laurel had gone past that and into the numbness stage a while ago. Or maybe she'd just been numb all along, ever since their father had left Mom high and dry, working two jobs to make ends meet, sacrificing any sort of personal life for her kids' comfort. Tanner, Parker and Laurel had needed to grow up fast. She herself had girded herself against so-called romance early, only letting Steve in. If she'd had trust issues before he had come along, she sure had a thousand more now.

Tanner had heard about every bit of it, too. He, along with Parker, had been her big, loving brother.

Laurel got out of her chair, sitting on the edge of her desk, wanting Tanner to see that she could walk away from that phone and the conversation she'd been having on it—that she was the independent woman she'd always wanted to be.

"I realized last night that I want to have some *fun,* Tanner," she said. "I've missed fun so much. I really haven't gotten out lately, and when I did last night, it occurred to me that it'd be great to have a guy around. It doesn't have to be anything serious. I grew up with a lot of males—you, Parker—and I've been around them ever since. I'm used to them. I miss them, too, but not in a…"

She was about to say "romantic way," but Tanner was already gripping the iPad, his knuckles white.

She went over to him, resting her hand on his, and he finally loosened up.

"I'm never going to forget what Steve did to me," she said. "So don't worry."

"I don't have to tell you to be careful, then?"

"I'm always careful. You know that better than anyone."

And she meant it, even if she was going on a picnic tomorrow with Sawyer Fortune, the playboy of his family.

The kind of man she would never, ever get serious with.

Chapter Three

Sawyer should've known that Laurel would be just as skilled in a saddle as she was in a cockpit.

By the time midmorning had rolled around, she'd bonded with her gray American Quarter horse, Old Smokey, guiding him over the riding trails on the New Fortunes Ranch just as if she knew where each path led. And when they arrived at the creek where he'd planned to stop for their brunch, she didn't need to be told how to loosen Old Smokey's girth or how to tether him to a nearby cottonwood.

After he took care of his paint, Lone Star, they unpacked their saddlebags. Laurel spread a plaid blanket over the ground as he brought out the picnic Carmen had packed for them: thermoses of coffee and orange juice, a fruit salad and breakfast baguette sandwiches with goat cheese, bacon and arugula.

Sawyer poured the juice into the mugs as Laurel fixed

their plates. Meanwhile, the creek water burbled by, the cottonwoods lending shade from the morning summer sun, the horses nickering in the near distance.

"Will Carmen be around after our ride so I can thank her for this?" Laurel asked, sitting with her legs to the side. Her long blond braid hung over a shoulder, and she was wearing a light blue shirt with a bit of lace at the scooped collar. She was so feminine, even with the cut muscles of her arms testifying that she was as athletic as they came.

"She should be," Sawyer said. "Carmen keeps the house tidy, too. She calls herself my backup mom."

"And your real mom? Is she anything like Carmen, cooking and cleaning for you?"

Sawyer laughed. "Her talents are better put to use in other areas. She went back to school recently for her degree."

"Good for her."

He was about to ask about Laurel's mom—her entire family, too—but she changed the subject. Intentionally? Sawyer wasn't sure.

"Thanks for bringing me out here," she said. "I can't believe I've lived in Texas for about a year and I haven't stopped to smell the roses like this. I needed it."

"You seem like a busy person."

"I like to stay that way, but wherever I've lived or traveled, I usually enjoy taking in the culture."

Sawyer scooped some fruit salad onto his fork. "What's your favorite country that you spent time in?"

"Oh, that's like asking me what my favorite book is, or my favorite movie—I have lists and can never choose a number one." She shrugged. "But I liked being stationed in Germany quite a bit. Cologne was great. It has a big cathedral that I loved to just stare at, plus ancient churches. Romans settled there over two thousand years ago, and they left their mark."

She must be a trivia buff. "Germany. I've been there, but it was a long time ago, right after I got out of college. I took one of those grand tours, backpacking style."

"With a friend?"

"Yeah. My college roommate. But we made a few more friends along the way, especially in the beer halls."

"What a surprise. Would I be wrong if I said that they were probably buddies of the female persuasion?"

It was Sawyer's turn to shrug. He didn't answer, just grinned and bit into his sandwich.

Laurel didn't seem to mind, though, as she stretched her legs in front of her, balancing her plate on her thighs and planting her hands on the ground. She was echoing his own posture, except she was raising her face to the branch-covered sky while he was watching *her*.

Sawyer enjoyed that she was enjoying herself. And he also appreciated that he could just hang out with a woman like this—no expectations, no pressure, no dealing with questions about whether there were strings attached to this time they were spending together.

But who was he fooling? She was more of a challenge than any woman he had encountered before, and that was part of the appeal.

A huge part.

As Laurel sighed, sat up straight and nibbled at her sandwich, his belly went tight. Even the way she chewed was sexy.

After she swallowed, she said, "You really picked a good spot to settle down on."

Settle down? Her turn of phrase made him grin. He'd already told her that he would never settle down.

"One of the things that drew me to Red Rock was how much land is available," he said. "I can have as many horses as I want here. I can ride them in any direction and it feels like the world is a million miles away."

She was watching him with a small smile, and he saw the same appreciation in her blue gaze—a need to get away from it all, whether you were half the globe away from home or right smack-dab in the middle of it.

"You're lucky," she said. "To have time enough to ride and lollygag on this ranch, I mean."

He recalled what she'd said the other night about him never having to work for anything.

Holding his juice mug, he didn't drink from it. He just stared at the creek trickling by. "You were right when you said that things have come easily to me. I really don't have to work. Partly because I'm a Fortune."

"And what's the other part?"

He wasn't sure. What was he besides a Fortune?

"Well," he said, "back when I was doing publicity and marketing for JMF Financial, I invested everything I earned carefully. Even without an inheritance, I'm a pretty wealthy person."

She laughed at his bluntness. "Not that you're bragging or anything."

"I'm not. It's just that it's simple to make money when you already have money. I *am* very lucky, just like you said."

She acknowledged all of that, then kept on eating, picking a piece off her baguette.

Did she think he was a rich, spoiled Fortune brat? She wasn't acting like it, taking what he was saying in stride. Strange, because he'd never been able to say serious things like this to a woman.

After she swallowed the bread, she said, "I'd be insanely envious of you if I didn't know all that gossip about your dad and him giving away half of JMF's majority shares to...what's her name? Jeanne Marie?"

"Yeah. Even rich people can be dysfunctional, huh?"

"You guys just get more publicity about it."

They laughed again, because it was true.

Was there anyone easier to talk to than Laurel Redmond? Ironic, seeing as that she hadn't let many guys at Mendoza's get a word out before she had them turning tail and going the other way.

An odd warmth rotated in his chest at the thought that she'd deemed him worthy of getting past her barriers.

He picked up his sandwich. "So it sounds like my family's probably not the only one with weird dynamics."

She'd been about to take a sip of orange juice, and she paused with the mug halfway to her lips, continuing after a second. It was as if drinking had given her an extra couple of seconds to formulate a response.

"I suppose," she said, after putting her drink down, "I could write a book on family dysfunction. My father— and I use the term loosely—hasn't shown his face since he walked out on us more than twenty years ago."

At least Sawyer had a father, faults and all. "I'm sorry to hear that. It must've been rough."

"I can't help thinking we got the good end of the deal."

She brushed the whole thing off, just as if the topic were a heap of crumbs on the picnic blanket.

Why did he get the feeling that she was putting on some kind of act, though? Had it been the too-cool tone of her voice? The way she was acting just a little more casual than most people would've?

Miss Independence, he thought. Had she become that way because her dad had set her attitude in motion long ago?

Before they could talk any more about it, she changed the subject again, just as she had earlier when they'd been discussing moms.

"This really was a great idea, Sawyer. I almost hate to go back to work tomorrow."

"Play hooky." He grinned.

"So says the billionaire."

"I'm serious. Why not?"

She was looking at him as if he came from another universe. "Because if I cancel the charter flights I have, business will go elsewhere. I'm still establishing a client base. Besides, today was only the first meeting of the Red Rock singleton club, right? We can have, say, one a month."

"I've got a birthday this Sunday," he said, not letting her off the hook that easily. "We should have another meeting to celebrate it. My brothers are throwing a small cocktail party for my big two-eight and—"

She picked up her napkin and tossed it at him, laughing. "No *way!*"

For a second, he thought he'd overstepped with her.

Until her laughter really kicked in.

"My birthday's Monday," she finally said. "Madame Luna should've told us we're almost twins."

Two of a kind, he thought again. He'd already known it, just as Laurel had known his number right off the bat.

"Then you're not getting out of that cocktail party," he said. "We'll celebrate your birthday, too, but just a little early."

He didn't add that having her at the small-scale party the night before his parents would be returning to town would take his mind off more troubles.

She'd gone quiet, her gaze on the creek, pensive. Was this where she was going to tell him that she'd changed her mind? That he was going places with her she hadn't asked for?

Sawyer was done being coy. And he supposed that Laurel was too much of a straight shooter for them to talk around this anymore.

"I'm gonna lay this out there," he said. "I like being around you, Laurel."

Her gaze was on the blanket now. "Same here. I'm having a great time. But I meant it when I said that I don't do relationships."

Why don't you? he wanted to ask. *Because of your father and how he left you and your family?*

He got the feeling there was more to it than even that.

But, like her, *he* didn't get in too deep, so he refrained from digging.

"I wasn't blowing smoke about being single and loving it, either," he said.

"So what're you saying? That we should be single together? Friends with benefits?"

A straight shooter, all right, and her naked comment got him right in the gut. He burned for her there, imagining her silky hair running through his fingers, her mouth under his...

He had to know. "If it's a bad idea, then just tell me. But I have to say that I don't find many women who aren't aiming for marriage, and it's a relief that you're not."

"Right," she said softly. "Never marriage."

Her voice was bolstered by a conviction so strong that he studied her a little more. She met his gaze, and hers was a liquid blue that made his blood rush through him.

It was clear that they were on the same page about everything.

"What if I kissed you," he asked, "just to see how it might work out?"

She didn't say anything, but he took that as a good sign, because he could see that she wanted a kiss.

A kiss would tell him what she was made of: Was she a woman of the world or just a girl who talked tough? A singleton who could put her money where her mouth was or a closet romantic who had told herself that she wasn't looking for love when she actually was?

When she leaned toward him, he was pulled toward her, too, by some force within himself. And when her eyes closed, her thick lashes like wispy fans on her tanned skin, his heart gave a tiny leap that made him wonder where it'd been all these years.

Their lips touched softly, but deep inside Sawyer, there was a hard thud of longing that rocked him.

A brush of the mouths, an inhalation that chopped

through him as she pulled away, as if she'd only wanted to test him.

His lips tingled. And Sawyer had never tingled there before.

She was breathy when she whispered, "I think that's a good sign."

Even now, he could feel her words on his lips, because they were still within an inch of each other. He could feel the warmth of her skin suffusing his face.

"*Is* it a good one?" he asked. "Because I could imagine even better signs between us."

She laughed, a bare sound that she covered up by angling away from him, then grabbing her plate. The shift in atmosphere was so abrupt that he didn't move.

What'd just happened?

It seemed that she wasn't nearly as affected as he'd been.

"As much as I'd love to while away the day here," she said, "I've got to get home. Paperwork, you know? It never ends."

He almost said that she'd told him she had the day off, but he didn't push it.

She'd kissed him, he thought, watching her as she went about her business as efficiently as she went about life, and although a kiss wasn't nearly enough, he'd take it for now.

When Laurel got home, the first thing she did was hit the shower.

It wasn't just because she smelled like horse—she needed something cold to douse the flames that were consuming her from the inside out.

But under the spray of water, under the streams of icy liquid that wiggled down her skin like fingers caressing her, she didn't get much relief.

Her rogue thoughts kept imagining that the water was Sawyer's fingers, Sawyer's lips, Sawyer, Sawyer, Sawyer...

Blowing out a breath, she got out of the stall, throwing on a robe and tying the belt around her waist.

You can't let him in, she thought. *He'll tear you apart before you know it, so don't even start getting close to him. Just keep it fun.*

But that shouldn't be a problem, because Sawyer didn't want a relationship, right? And wasn't that perfect? Wasn't that what every trigger-shy woman needed—a hottie to warm her up whenever she wanted, but without any consequences?

Theirs was just a chemical attraction, she told herself. And that's all it would ever amount to....

The phone rang and she dashed to it, thankful for something to take her mind off him.

The ID screen revealed good news and bad.

The good? It was Juliet, her best friend since college.

The bad? Juliet was the person who'd introduced her to Steve Lucas and was a constant reminder of him, even if Laurel didn't blame her friend for what had happened with him.

But Juliet always felt the need to apologize, and Laurel didn't want the sorries; she just wanted her friend back, the way they'd been before the whole Steve thing had gone down.

She answered the phone. "Hey there."

"Hey, yourself," Juliet echoed in her Oklahoma drawl.

"Thomas and I are at Brew Hah Hah's and I just had to call."

Brew Hah Hah's was the big hangout near campus at the University of Oklahoma, where Laurel had won a full-ride scholarship. Juliet and her husband had gone there this weekend just to relive some old times, she told Laurel.

"Drink one for me, okay?" Laurel said.

"Already have." Juliet didn't exactly hiccup, but her giggle was revealing. "What're you up to?"

Laurel hadn't talked to Juliet since she'd met Sawyer. Actually, Laurel hadn't met *any* guys worth mentioning to her best friend, and that had been a good thing. Juliet was worse than Tanner and Parker when it came to telling Laurel to be careful.

She sucked it up and spilled it out. "I went horseback riding today."

"Cool!"

"With a guy."

"With…a guy. Ah." Big pause. "What's his name?"

Juliet was already in hovering-hen mode.

"Sawyer," Laurel said. "And before you start a background check, you should know that it's nothing serious."

"It's not?"

"No. We're…casual."

Not serious. Casual. How many times would she repeat those words when it came to Sawyer?

Juliet had hesitated again, and Laurel could almost see her friend twirling a strand of her auburn hair around a finger, a nervous habit.

"Don't misunderstand me," she finally said. "I want

you to get out there, Laurel, have some fun. God knows you stopped having it when…well, when Steve wiped you out."

Just the reminder made Laurel close her eyes, but she forced herself to open them. She rested her back against the wall, across from the framed pictures of herself and her buddies in and out of uniform, hanging out in Berlin, Frankfurt, even at the Kandahar airfield.

Her past hadn't been all bad. She reminded herself of that every day, too.

Juliet continued. "Who is this Sawyer, anyway?"

A Fortune. A rascal. A man who made her tummy flip even though she tried to hide that fact with a cool attitude.

"He's got money," Laurel said. "And I'm telling you that because it means he won't rob me blind."

But she'd only trusted Steve because she'd been in love, and because she thought that there couldn't be anyone on earth nearly as crappy as her father. Steve had proven her wrong.

Juliet sighed. "I'm sorry I even *ask* these questions, Laurel. But I did such a crummy job of judging Steve. He passed my best-friend tests, he was Thomas's pal at work and he was a civilian pilot whom I thought you'd have a lot in common with. Never in a thousand years did I think—"

"None of us did, Jules."

Why did most of their conversations have to end this way?

Laurel didn't want to dwell on Steve, so she changed the subject back to Brew Hah Hah's, letting Juliet talk about new beers they had on tap and how the students just weren't the same as they used to be back when *they* went to college.

Hadn't she done the same thing a couple of times with Sawyer earlier? Changed the subject when they'd landed on the topic of her family?

As Juliet kept talking, Laurel's mind drifted back to Sawyer. Back to their kiss.

And her head stayed there, chasing her troubles away for at least the time being.

If Laurel hadn't been out of town the next few days, flying chartered flights, she might've found it easier to contain herself at the idea of seeing Sawyer again.

As it was, thoughts of him bubbled in her whenever she had a spare moment.

The minute her feet touched the ground in Red Rock on Saturday, she headed for her office, where she planned to call Sawyer about that small cocktail party he'd talked about for his birthday. Actually, she wanted to talk her way *out* of attending tomorrow.

For one, his family would be there, and friends with benefits didn't do intimate family gatherings. Two, she wasn't sure she had a dress nice enough for cocktails with the Fortunes, even if most of them ran around Red Rock in jeans and boots nowadays.

When she opened the door to the office, she got the surprise of her life, her breath jamming in her lungs.

Sawyer?

Seated in her desk chair, he looked perfectly at home, his brown hair tousled as if he'd just gotten out of the shiny red Jaguar convertible everyone said he drove around, speeding above the limit with the top down.

He was also reading one of the three books she always had on hand.

He lifted it up so the cover faced her. It was a book of essays that analyzed the effects that popular fiction had on society. "Very informative, Laur."

There was that *Laur* again, and she was liking the sound of it more and more from him.

"It's a good read," she said, tossing her flight bag onto a nearby chair, giving him a what-the-hell-are-you-doing-here look.

He could obviously read her as well as any book. In a lot of ways, anyway.

"I'm just thinking about the significance of your literary choices," he said. "You could be reading actual fun, popular-literature books, but instead, you're choosing to read *about* them."

She hadn't thought about it that deeply, but now that he mentioned it, she *was* a fairly analytical person.

"I listen to my fun stuff on audio," she said in her defense.

He cocked an eyebrow, put that book down and gestured to her other two, a sociological rumination on why people could be rude and a book on healthy eating.

Analytical, analytical.

"Stimulating stuff," he said. "I'll bet you read that *Fifty Shades* book at night, though."

"Wouldn't you like to know?"

He grinned that sexy grin that had won her over at Mendoza's—a tickle to her heart, a trickle of heat winding through her belly.

Damn, she was ridiculously happy to see him. *Too* happy.

She crossed her arms over her chest, but that didn't work, because she couldn't help smiling at him.

"So what brings you here, Fortune? Did you schedule a flying lesson with another pilot today?"

"No." He leaned back in her chair and folded his hands behind his head, making him look even sexier. "I'm in dire need of a woman's touch."

Had he just said…?

He laughed at her silence. "What I mean is that I need some help picking out wedding gifts for my brothers and their soon-to-be wives, and I thought of you."

Okay, that made more sense. "That's right—the wedding is in a couple of weeks."

"I was on my way to San Antonio when I realized that I had no earthly idea what to get them. So I called here, and Max Allen told me that you were due in around this time."

"No one has ever accused me of being a shopper before, Fortune. Are you sure I'm the girl for this job?"

"I'll take my chances."

His words had all kinds of meaning, but she didn't— no, *wouldn't*—latch onto any one of them.

But she couldn't help wondering…was this the start of their friends-with-benefits time?

Her body roared with the hope that it was.

She calmed herself down. No way was he going to see what she was really feeling.

"Do you have any ideas whatsoever for those gifts?" she asked.

"I really don't. But I thought if you wanted to come with me to check out a department store or two, that would get me going."

Another innuendo? Because just the sound of his voice, the sight of him and his wickedly gleaming blue eyes were enough to get *her* going.

Besides, it wasn't as if she'd planned to do anything tonight. Just another Saturday evening in front of the TV, reading, eating something she'd picked up from the market and going to bed early. If she hadn't met Sawyer, she might've even ended up at Mendoza's again, telling herself she couldn't possibly feel lonely in the middle of a crowd.

He stood. "So what do you say? I'll even take you out for a birthday dinner."

"If that means I don't have to go to that cocktail party with your family tomorrow, then I'm game."

He held a hand to his chest. "You wound me, Laur."

"I just..." She shrugged. "People like us don't go to family functions. Know what I mean?"

People like us. Friends with could-be benefits.

His gaze darkened with something she thought might be yearning. Just the possibility of it sent her adrenaline racing, her blood rolling.

"Besides," she said, "Tanner's taking me out to lunch tomorrow to celebrate while we have a day off, so my schedule's kind of full."

"Even with lunch, you'll still have a lot of time before cocktails."

She wanted to toss up her hands in exasperation. "Do you think you'll get your way on this? Because it's not going to happen, Fortune."

He smiled, as if she was going to find out she was wrong eventually. As if he always got what he wanted.

And that was probably true.

He came out from behind the desk, six feet tall and dressed in those muscle-hugging jeans, brushing past her with his leathery scent and stopping at the door, holding it open for her and grinning.

Her legs had gone weak.

The question wasn't what he would talk her into doing tomorrow, she thought. It was what he might get her to do tonight.

Chapter Four

He'd gotten his way, all right.

Laurel had indeed come with him, sitting in his Jag convertible without making excuses or telling him to take a hike after he'd unexpectedly shown up in the flight-school office.

But just how easy was Laurel, really?

That very question stimulated Sawyer as he got behind the wheel and took off from the airport parking lot to the road, where he put pedal to the metal all the way to San Antonio with the radio playing loud country music.

Stray blond hair from her braid flew in the wind as she leaned her head back, her sunglasses on, a smile on her face as she rested her arm on the top of the door where the window was down.

It looked as if she was flying high, the speed and the all-encompassing air taking her to a better place.

But what did she want to escape? Her dysfunctional family?

Or more, as he'd suspected the other day at the picnic?

When they got to San Antonio, he pulled into an upscale shopping complex in the North Central part of the city and gave the Jag over to the valet.

"Where to now?" Laurel asked, sliding her sunglasses to the top of her head. She'd rolled the sleeves of her white linen shirt to her elbows and untucked it, tying it at the waist of her khakis. She came off as someone who didn't have to try hard to be stylish. She wasn't even wearing more than a light coat of lipstick, as far as he could tell.

Still, she was a knockout.

He pushed back his rogue hair that'd been tossed around by the wind. "We're going to Hurston's. I figure there's bound to be something there my brothers will like."

"But not anything they'll need."

She smiled at him, and he gave her the point.

They walked into the second-floor entrance, through the cosmetics and perfume section. He couldn't help but notice that Laurel didn't linger over the counters; she didn't even cast a moony glance over to the left, where he caught a peek of a secluded room that contained the flash of diamonds.

Most women would've dropped about fifty hints to him by now about those shiny necklaces and bracelets. *How do you think this would look on me, Sawyer? This... and nothing else, if you know what I mean...*

But Laurel didn't play those games. She was on a

mission, headed for the escalators, passing a man in a black suit playing an old standard on a baby grand piano.

Sawyer joined her at the store map and they surveyed the departments.

"Any thoughts?" he asked.

"You know your brothers better than I do."

"But you were right earlier when you said they don't *need* anything. I suppose I should be thinking about what they *want*."

He noticed that, off to the side, near the high-end women's department, a few ladies in elegant suits and chignons were giving him and Laurel the once-over. He counted down to how long it'd take one of them to put a name to his face.

And five...four...three...

A woman with black hair and a red designer suit made a beeline toward him, leaving her coworkers in the dust.

"Good afternoon," she said in a refined drawl. "My name is Jasmine. Is there anything I can help you with?"

He could feel Laurel sneaking a glance at him, gauging his reaction to the beauty queen. But he just wasn't interested.

Not in Jasmine, anyway.

He said, "We're shopping for a wedding."

"Oh."

She sounded slightly disappointed by that, and Sawyer realized that she thought he was talking about a wedding for him and Laurel, who was back to surveying the store map.

Had she been paying attention to his exchange with the salesclerk? From her nonreaction, he guessed she hadn't.

This might be fun.

Jasmine had a very professional smile on her red-shaded mouth, her dark eyes all but filled with dollar signs now. "Which department would you like to see first, Mr...."

"Fortune."

"Of course, yes, I knew it was you. Your family is in the papers quite a bit."

Before she could launch into a gossip-column item about all the charity events he'd ever attended with a society belle on his arm—or, God forbid, the Jeanne Marie scandal—Laurel smoothly walked between Sawyer and Jasmine, giving him a subtle nudge.

"I think," she said to Jasmine, "we'd like to concentrate on a travel package—items you'd pack for, say, a tropical vacation for a husband and wife."

Well played, he thought as he followed Laurel away from the escalators and toward the women's department. He could give Asher, Wyatt and Shane and their fiancées suitcases filled with hints about where he could send them on romantic trips after they finished their official honeymoons.

Jasmine was all over that, her heels clicking on the marble floor as she took the lead in front of Laurel, who shot him an amused smile. He still wasn't sure she'd heard Jasmine mistake this shopping trip for their own wedding spree, though.

Laurel hung back with Sawyer as Jasmine slipped around the racks of women's wear, targeting the most expensive section near the back.

"Do you know what sizes your future sisters-in-law take?" Laurel whispered.

"I'll find out. We can just look for now and, if we see anything we like, I'm sure Jasmine will accommodate us later."

"Accommodate *you*." Laurel stifled a laugh.

Lightheartedly, he cupped his hand on her nape, squeezing. He'd meant it to be a joking gesture, but when he felt a shock zapping him from his fingers to his chest, he let go.

Did she feel it, too?

From the way she nearly lost a step, he thought so. But she recovered so quickly that he wasn't sure.

Either way, his pulse took him over, beating in his ears, his belly.

Jasmine had stopped in front of a purple satin-curtained room—probably a boutique that held pricey goodies for women.

"I think," she said, "you'll find all kinds of things in here for a tropical vacation for a bride and groom."

Laurel went in first, but he wasn't far behind. And when he saw all the lace and silk, his libido banged up another notch, because he immediately started picturing her in the pink baby-doll number to his right.

As for Laurel, she widened her eyes at him. *What the hell?*

"Clearly," Jasmine said, "you'll want some items for the bride's trousseau."

Sawyer decided to make the most of the situation, and he reached over to a sheer, charcoal-gray bodysuit with flowers covering the strategic spots.

"What do you think, honey?" he asked. "Is there anything in here that pulls your trigger?"

Laurel, who was never at a loss for words, sure was

this time as she sent a bemused glance around the room. But that only gave his fantasy machine time to get to work on picturing her in the bodysuit.

Long legs, slim hips, that slender waist, breasts barely hidden by the floral appliqués, her long blond hair raining over him as she crawled onto their bed and slid her body up his...

Jasmine had come over to pluck the bodysuit off the wall and hold it out to him. "It's beautiful, isn't it? La Perla." She turned to Laurel. "You would look fantastic in this."

"Me?"

Okay. She definitely hadn't heard Jasmine back by the escalators when the salesclerk had assumed that they'd be shopping for *their* wedding.

"Yes, you," Jasmine said, starting to walk toward Laurel with the lingerie outstretched, as if sizing her. "And charcoal works very well with your coloring."

For a moment, it seemed as if Laurel was picturing herself in the lingerie, her gaze going that dreamy shade he'd seen before whenever she talked about flying.

But then she held up her hands. "Whoa, wait. Did you say...? No. *We're* not getting married."

The expression she wore was so incredulous that she didn't even have to say *I'm never getting married. Are you kidding?*

"I mean," she continued, "there's a wedding, but..."

As she looked to Sawyer for an assist, he just grinned.

But then he took pity on her. "What she means, Jasmine, is that we're shopping for someone else, and maybe we should concentrate on resort wear or something like that."

Jasmine put a hand to her chest, contrite. "I'm so sorry. I thought…"

Her attitude seemed to change in a heartbeat, from embarrassed to intrigued, and she ran a gaze over Sawyer.

Laurel certainly caught onto *that,* and he thought he saw her roll her eyes before she turned toward the exit and went outside.

Good God, did she think that he was going to hit on another woman while he was out with her? Sure, this wasn't an official date, but her slight opinion of him stung.

He got out his wallet and took out several hundred-dollar bills. He also fetched a generic business card with his personal assistant's information on it. Mrs. Deaver was in Atlanta, but even though Sawyer hadn't been in the office for a while, he still used her services.

"You estimated her size, right?" he asked, nodding toward the door where Laurel had disappeared.

Jasmine went back to being all business again. "Yes, Mr. Fortune."

"Then I'd like you to pick out a cocktail dress for her, with matching shoes, accessories, the works. My assistant will give you an address for the delivery."

Jasmine must've realized that even if there wasn't a wedding going on with him and Laurel, that didn't mean *nothing* was going on.

"Certainly, Mr. Fortune. I'll take care of this right away."

"Thanks. I'll have my assistant work with you on those wedding gifts, too." He'd given her enough money for a generous tip, as well.

One more thing, though.

"And that?" He gestured to the bodysuit she was still holding. "Send it with the cocktail dress, would you?"

He wanted Laurel to not only be prepared for that party tomorrow evening…he wanted her to be ready for anything.

If the chemistry between them was any indication, he doubted they'd be stopping at a kiss tonight.

Laurel had busied herself in the women's sportswear section while Sawyer did whatever he was doing with Jasmine.

Was he putting the moves on her? Taking a moment to multitask as he kept one woman out here and another in the lingerie boutique?

She whipped through some bathing suit wraps, the hangers clacking over the bar. Why should she care what he did with Jasmine? It wasn't as if she and Sawyer were on a date.

So why was she jealous?

She stopped in the middle of a hanger swipe. Yikes. She *was* jealous. The whole time, while she'd been keeping an eye on Jasmine, seeing how the woman would sneak a glance at Sawyer and smile to herself, she'd been burning up inside.

But what girl wouldn't? He was gorgeous and charming and…

Halting midlist, Laurel told herself to chill out. No need to get emotional when emotions were the last thing that applied to her and Sawyer.

Casual, she repeated. *No attachments. Just fun.*

When he came out of the lingerie boutique, he spotted her, his blue eyes lighting up. She hadn't expected that, and it felt like a tiny elevator had rushed up from her belly to her chest, carrying all sorts of baggage.

"Sorry for the delay," he said, coming to stand next to her.

She breathed in the scent of leather. He always smelled so good.

"Did you finish your business with Jasmine?" she asked, trying for an offhanded tone.

Fail.

He chuckled, resting his fingertips on her upper arm. The patch of skin where he connected to her pulsed.

"I was making a few arrangements," he said. "That's all. Now that you gave me that idea for the wedding gifts, I'm off and running."

She moved away from the clothing, walking through the other racks. "All right, then. Looks like we're done here."

"Were you embarrassed?" he asked, stopping her. "When Jasmine assumed that we were getting married, you seemed like it. I'm sorry if that's the case."

What could she say? That for a dizzy moment, she'd seen how Sawyer had looked at her, as if imagining her in that bodysuit? That her stomach had twisted and her breath had been cut short?

That she'd started imagining what it might be like, in that lingerie, in a dim room, with him looking at her the exact same way…?

She shrugged off his apology, as well as the encroaching fantasy.

"I wasn't embarrassed," she said.

He didn't argue with her, even if she suspected that he knew she'd gotten flustered.

When they came to the garage, they had the valet retrieve the Jag, and before Sawyer took off, he turned to her.

"You hungry yet?"

She was. Then again, she always had an appetite. "I could do with some food."

"Great." He got out his phone, texted something, then returned the device to his shirt pocket.

"Where are we going?" she asked. "I'm afraid I'm only dressed nicely enough for fast food."

"This is for your birthday, Laur. Trust me."

He wheeled the Jag out of the parking structure, and it wasn't too much later that they arrived downtown at the River Walk, which featured a bank of shops, restaurants and bars that lined the water.

As they strolled down the walkway, he put his hand at the small of her back to guide her under the trees and evening-shaded lamps toward a restaurant on the water.

At the feel of him, she slowed down, and it wasn't only because her nerve endings were sparking. The restaurant looked fancy, with a waterfall splashing outside.

"This is too nice, Sawyer. I'm not—"

"Dressed for it. Don't worry—you always look amazing."

She glanced at him, and she could see that he wasn't just giving her a line. There was something about his gaze, an intensity, that made her glance away and vibrate that much more.

They entered the restaurant, which was lit through and through by reflections from the pools around the room—waves of light on the ceiling, sleek aquariums near the booths and tables, angelic fish with fragile fins swimming in the water.

This was damned romantic.

"Sawyer..."

"Come on," he said, grabbing her by the hand and following the maître d' as he headed toward an elevator, which took them upstairs.

All the while, Sawyer held her hand. And she didn't remove it, liking the feel of his fingers wrapped over hers.

Warm all over, hormones coming alive...

The friends-with-benefits stage was really starting, was it?

They ended up in a private dining room that overlooked the River Walk's paths and the water. A wall-sized tank featured lionfish, giving the room an under-the-sea atmosphere.

The maître d' left menus and a wine list with them, then announced that their waiter would be there soon.

Laurel pointed at Sawyer. "You texted them to open the private dining room."

"Anything for the birthday girl."

"You barely know me, and already you've given me too much."

"What? A dinner?" Sawyer looked at the menu as if to ignore her comment, but that devilish smile tipped the corners of his mouth. "You're not used to expecting what you deserve, Laur."

Her? She thought about that while Sawyer passed her the wine list, as if she deserved any vintage on it.

All her life, she hadn't ever expected to deserve anything, and he was making her think she might've been wrong about that.

She looked at the wine list, almost sucking in her breath at the prices. But she'd had a lot of wine in her time, in a lot of places. After she'd finished active duty in Afghanistan, she'd done a bit of traveling, deciding to live near Tanner and his family, traveling some more, then laying her flight bag down in Red Rock.

So she picked a dry white Côtes du Rhône blend from eastern France that wasn't too expensive, but not cheap, either.

The waiter came to the table, greeting them, asking if they cared for wine or a cocktail.

Sawyer nodded to her, giving her leave to order whatever she wanted.

She gave their waiter her choice, and he approved.

"Wonderful with the oysters with chorizo," the waiter said. "May I suggest the hors d'asparagus to start off?"

They agreed with the waiter on his recommendation, and he left them to the blue-lit room and the darkened sky outside the window.

"Just look at this place," she said. "You've got good taste."

"Good to hear that. I think you're not so easily impressed. You've experienced a lot."

"Not really." Besides, she *was* impressed with him. He was turning out to be a gentleman. That wouldn't matter in the end, after their benefits ran out, but she could appreciate what he brought to the table now.

"And you call *me* prepared," she said. "Texting was a good trick."

"I've been here more than a few times, and I know what the restaurant has to offer."

"More than a few times, huh? With how many women?"

It'd come out unchecked, but she'd been wondering, hadn't she? Why not ask?

Sawyer leaned back in his chair, entertained. "So you *are* curious."

"Just as curious as you probably are about me."

Ooh—he obviously liked that answer. She could tell by his wry grin.

"All right," he said. "I've brought at least five women here, but with all those damned Fortune weddings going on, Texas has been like a second home to me. I've had time for more than a few dates."

"And not one of them stuck?" she asked. "You didn't bring any of those women here a second time?"

He shook his head.

"Really?" she asked, softer now. "You've never had anyone who…lasted?"

"No. But that's okay. You know how I feel about the whole lasting thing."

"Yes, I do."

A pause dragged by, and thank God for their waiter, because that's when he came with the wine.

After he'd poured it and left the bottle in an ice bucket, Laurel got the feeling Sawyer was about to ask about all the men she'd brought to the places she'd enjoyed.

And…yup.

"You've been in love," he said. "I can tell by the way you're trying so hard not to talk about it."

There was no getting around this, so she did one of

two things that she always did whenever she had to talk about her dad or anything painful. And she had the feeling that Sawyer wouldn't let her change the subject this time.

So she only shrugged, acting as if Steve didn't matter.

"I was in love once," she said. "But I'm afraid my story isn't all that interesting."

"Try me."

He was watching her with such intensity that she almost lost every word that was bunched in her throat, but she cleared it, recovering.

"I got to know a guy through mutual friends and we developed a relationship online," she said. "Steve Lucas. He was a private pilot, and we had a lot in common. We emailed each other every day, and we met each other whenever I was in the U.S. I'd always been too busy to have anyone in my life, and I'm afraid I was really naive about love."

"What did he do to you?"

Laurel wrestled with telling him. She didn't want anyone feeling sorry for her, most of all Sawyer. But he'd been honest with her, and she respected that enough to return the favor.

"We'd been dating for a while—months—but to me it seemed like forever. I trusted him as much as I would my brothers. Or my best friend, who, by the way, gave him her thumbs-up, since Steve knew her husband from work. So when he suggested that we merge our bank accounts and then move in together—he said he'd come and be with me wherever I was—I didn't think much of it. I was going to marry him, even after I'd seen what my dad did to my mom."

"You loved him that much."

"I did."

Sawyer looked down, as if he knew what was coming.

She kept her voice level, removed. "So we did the joint bank accounts and about a week later, he and my money were gone."

Sawyer shook his head. "I'm sorry, Laur."

"You're sorry?" She laughed, just to make it seem like it was nothing. "I was the dumb one. I should've learned from my mother's experiences. Instead I had to learn from my own."

"Sadder but wiser," he said softly, but there was no pity there, just an understanding. "Did he ever get caught?"

"Not because of me. Before I could press charges, someone else put the hammer down on him—an ex-girlfriend. I never knew about her but, evidently, all those months, she'd had the law collecting enough evidence to finally sting him. It was good timing, but it didn't make me feel any better."

Sawyer was giving her one of those long glances again, and she felt as if he was trying to see past the front she always put up.

And he was succeeding moment by moment, winding his way into her.

But that couldn't happen, and she looked away, lifting her wineglass and drinking, then smiling at him as if the conversation had never occurred.

She wasn't sure if he felt thwarted or not, because he merely picked up his wine, as well.

"Even after everything," he said, "you still came out a winner."

Yes, she had.

She just wasn't sure what she'd won yet.

Sawyer was sure that dinner had been terrific, but he couldn't actually remember tasting much of it, mostly because, for the first time with a woman, he'd been too absorbed with Laurel to notice anything else.

It was just that she brought new angles to every course, what with her worldly knowledge of different cultures.

She was more than fascinating. She was downright compelling, luring him with her spirit and her strength.

But was she so attractive to him because she embodied the independence he was looking for outside of the Fortune offices?

Or because of a reason he still wasn't sure about yet?

He drove her home, following the directions she'd provided to the modest side of town, where the apartments were well-kept brick affairs with manicured lawns. After he pulled into the parking lot and cut the engine, he turned to her, moonlight silvering her hair to an even lighter shade. His pulse went weak, as if floating in him.

"These are nice," he said, motioning toward the apartments.

"The ex-boyfriend didn't destroy my finances altogether."

"Do me a favor and don't mention him again," he said. "All I want to do is wrap my hands around that ass's throat."

She grinned. "Don't let him get to you. I make decent money now, thanks to Tanner. He helped me get back on my feet with a loan, and I've just about paid him off. Things are good."

He wanted to tell her that life could be even better. If she ever wanted money, he'd give it to her. But that smacked of what he was trying to escape in the first place with women. And Laurel wasn't like the others, because if he offered, she'd no doubt consider it a slap in the face.

"Well," she said, tucking a strand of hair behind her ear.

He wanted to kiss her, and she had to know it. Maybe she even wanted it just as badly.

When they locked gazes, he could see in her eyes that she did, and his pulse thudded through him.

He leaned over an inch, and she did, too.

Just a bit more, as she closed her eyes...

A dog barked from a path nearby and they drew away from each other. She laughed, but he didn't.

"I really had a great day," she said, back-to-normal Laurel, whom he suspected got embarrassed more easily than she would admit.

She opened the car door.

"Whoa," he said, getting out and circling behind the Jag. "That's my job."

She inclined her head, waiting for him until he'd opened her door all the way. He took her by the hand and helped her to her feet.

Again, they didn't make a move to end the night. Just like they'd done on the dance floor on their first meeting, he kept holding her fingers in his. But now, he whisked a thumb over hers, and she took in a breath.

And now, unlike at the picnic, he didn't stop to ask if she would allow him the pleasure.

He slid his hand to the back of her neck, her gaze going wide and soft.

"The day doesn't have to end yet, Laurel," he said, just before he lowered his mouth to hers.

Chapter Five

It was as if Laurel, who'd always believed so devoutly in structure, didn't have any of it as Sawyer's mouth pressed down on hers.

Her legs gave out first, making her dip back a little and, in response, making him wrap his arms around her to hold her up. Then her torso went liquid, filled with swamped heartbeats that sounded as if they were coming from underwater, far away.

Every one of those pulses echoed, traveling through her body as if she were a single, connected waterway, beats rolling through her like waves that pounded one right after another.

As if afraid of drowning in him, she grasped his shirt, dragging him toward her, slowing down the kiss, parting her lips until they sipped at each other, dizzy, hazy, spun-motion temptation.

Leather, she kept thinking. She couldn't get enough of

his scent, of his skin and his five o'clock shadow scraping her face, leaving a pleasant burn.

She buried a hand in his hair—thick and lustrous—bringing him closer to her, as close as he could get. Closer than she'd been to anyone in her whole life.

And it still wasn't enough.

When he stroked his tongue into her mouth, she held her breath, suspended on a crest of lazy desire. He stroked her again, then again, until a sensual rhythm consumed them, a sensuous pattern that had taken her over—in her chest, in her belly, between her legs.

Aching... How could she ache so much for anyone, just from a kiss?

Unable to get air into her lungs, she turned her head aside. He nuzzled her neck.

She was still reeling, clutching his shirt, nearly pulling it off him.

"I've been waiting to do that," he whispered against her skin.

"You did it the other day." She had no idea how she'd gotten the words out. "At the picnic."

He laughed and she felt it in his chest, felt the borrowed vibrations in her own chest.

"That wasn't a kiss at the picnic," he said. "*This* was a kiss."

Yeah, it had been.

He rubbed his mouth over her ear, and her knees buckled.

"Sweet spot?" he asked.

If only he knew how many of those she had. Hell, she suspected that with Sawyer Fortune, her whole body might be a sweet spot.

"Don't push it, cowboy," she said, her voice sounding drunk. "We're out in the middle of my parking lot."

"We can remedy that."

He lifted his hand, touched the place on her neck where his lips had been, caressing her lightly.

She might as well have not had any knees whatsoever, for all the good they were doing her right now. It felt as if the only thing binding her was a thin thread of what common sense she had left.

Was it common sense telling her not to rush in, though? Or did she just want to draw out these kisses? To be chased by Sawyer until one of them exploded with this lust that she couldn't deny anymore?

"Are you hinting about taking this to my apartment?" she asked.

"I can do more than hint."

She doubted she could withstand what he was thinking of doing to her next.

Lightly, she put a hand on his chest. "I'm sure you can manage a whole lot, Sawyer, but it won't be tonight."

He trailed a finger from the side of her neck to the cove where her collarbones met. Another sweet spot, and this time she made a tiny sound of delight.

"Really, Laurel?" he asked. "You want to call it a night?"

Nope. But that pesky common sense of hers had gotten stronger and was now clawing through all the desire.

And as she got her breath back, common sense started to *make* more sense.

She planted both hands against his chest now, a move that was meant to put the kibosh on all this, but…oh, man. Muscles. Skin.

What did he look like under that shirt?

Save it for later.

When she gave him a gentle push away, he laughed again, looking as if this had never happened before. A woman saying no.

But there was a first time for everything.

"'Night, cowboy."

And with all the gumption she had, she sauntered away from him. It would've been a fine show, too, if she'd remembered that she had her flight bag in the car.

Dammit.

She went back to get it, still acting like Josie Cool, even though she was more like Josie Hot and Bothered.

"I just forgot this," she said, smiling, holding up her bag, then backtracking toward the path to her apartment. Yes, very cool.

He'd come to lean against his convertible, his arms crossed loosely over his chest, a you'll-regret-this grin on his mouth.

More temptation.

More of a reason to get her butt to her apartment *alone*.

She turned all the way around, walking the path to safety, thinking she was fully in control now.

Until he spoke in that low, heart-pulsing drawl.

"Sleep tight, Laur."

"You bet I will."

He laughed as if he knew better.

And it turned out he did, because once she'd settled down and gotten ready for bed, sleep didn't come easy.

Neither did the return of her common sense, as her mind gave way to all the lingerie fantasies that had started earlier at the department store, when he'd just about burned her up with a desire-filled gaze.

Sawyer had gone home and taken a cold shower.
Ice-cold.

He'd hated to see the evening end, and not only because Laurel hadn't invited him in. The day after tomorrow was when his parents would be arriving in town, and he wasn't looking forward to the family fireworks.

But he still had his birthday to look forward to before they came, as well as a cocktail party that Laurel would hopefully be attending.

The next morning, after a restless night of sleep and after he'd contacted Mrs. Deaver about the shopping he'd done, he couldn't stop thinking of what Laurel would look like in whatever kind of dress Jasmine the salesclerk had picked out....

And whether Laurel would be wearing that bodysuit for him anytime soon.

The hours lumbered by for Sawyer as he made himself busy around the ranch, visiting with the foreman to see how the stables were running in particular, and taking a ride over the property to check the fences, just like a real cowboy would.

But there was something he'd started to realize since Laurel had appeared in his life—he hadn't actually come to Red Rock to play rancher. He'd begun to feel differently about the ranch in a way he couldn't identify yet.

When cocktail hour rolled around, Sawyer cleaned up and put on a suit. Usually, he avoided them like... well, the plague. But tonight he donned something that spoke to his casual yet tasteful needs a little better—a

tailored Hugo Boss ensemble that allowed him to skip
the tie but include the black jacket and trousers. He also
carefully combed back his hair, just to make it look like
he was putting out as much effort for this small party as
his brothers and sister had.

He drove a short way over the ranch road to a new
building that he'd had constructed just for the purpose
of socializing—a large, enclosed gazebo that would be
perfect for throwing soirees and barbecues.

And a wedding, he thought. His brothers' reception
was set to take place here.

A barbecue was already going outside the gazebo tonight, though, and as Sawyer pulled up to where some
other cars were parked, he could see a small catering
staff manning a couple of grills.

The smell of beef brisket floated on the air as he got
out of his car and glanced around. He wasn't sure what
Laurel drove, but all he saw were his family's rides.

His chest clenched—was she going to come tonight?
He'd texted her party details this morning, and all he'd
gotten back was a mysterious smiley face.

That was good, wasn't it?

Shane and Asher, who'd already shed their suit jack-
ets, were on the steps of the gazebo. Sawyer couldn't
see who was inside just yet.

"Birthday boy!" Shane said, welcoming Sawyer with
a hearty pat on the back.

Asher smiled at Sawyer, a beer in one hand. "Jace
says happy birthday, too. I told him I'd save him some
cake."

"I'll deliver it to him personally," Sawyer said.

His four-year-old nephew would just have to settle for

some birthday time with his uncle away from this cocktail hour. But Jace wouldn't mind—Sawyer had promised to celebrate with him at Six Flags soon.

Shane pushed him inside the gazebo. Sawyer saw his
brother Wyatt by the manned bar first, dressed in a suit
that looked more like something a rancher from the Old
West would wear than garb for a former VP of JMF Financial. He was pouring champagne into their younger
sister, Victoria's, flute. She looked as darling as ever,
with her curly brown hair flowing over her shoulders
and wearing a red, summery designer dress.

They cheerily wished Sawyer a happy birthday, too,
as everyone else got up from the tables to greet him:
Lia Serrano, Shane's fiancée, who was pregnant out to
here. Marnie McCafferty, Asher's intended. Sarah-Jane
Early, Wyatt's future wife. And last but never least, Garrett Stone, Victoria's cowboy husband.

Shane gestured around the room. "This was as small
as we could get it, Sawyer."

"Yeah." Wyatt smiled, his arm around Sarah-Jane.
"But no matter how many times Sawyer demands a low-
profile birthday party, I'm still surprised. He's supposed
to be our wild man."

"It's just another year to add to the rest," Sawyer said.

Lately he'd begun wondering if there was something
else to his dislike of big birthday shindigs. Had he always wanted to avoid drawing attention to the fact that
he hadn't accomplished as much as the rest of the Fortunes, year by year? That he hadn't gone much of anywhere in life from one birthday to the next?

Asher had nudged him toward the gift table. "Mom
wanted you to open her present first."

Of course their mother would've sent something ahead of her arrival tomorrow.

"Don't you mean her and Dad's gift?" Victoria asked.

Asher shrugged.

Wyatt spoke to his siblings. "Should we just tell him before he opens it?"

"Tell me what?" Sawyer asked.

Asher made a slightly embarrassed gesture as everyone else looked at Sawyer with sympathy. Great—was it going to be one of these nights?

"She'd planned to be here," Asher said. "She made arrangements when she called Victoria the other day, and it was supposed to be a surprise."

Shane said, "You know how we feel about Dad right now. We weren't sure you'd want him here, either, so we made it clear that he should probably seek a little forgiveness before strolling into a party as if nothing ever happened."

So his brothers had decided for Sawyer that their father wasn't welcome at this party. And why not? They didn't want him at their triple wedding, and they'd been the ones to plan things tonight.

Even so, Sawyer chafed a little at their presumption, even if they thought they were just looking out for him.

"It's okay," Sawyer said, blowing everything off with a smile that felt forced. "You guys are here. Mom tried to be. Life is good."

Everyone just stood there, as if they all knew that it really wasn't very okay.

But Victoria saved the moment.

"I'm supposed to call Mom when we sing 'Happy Birthday' so she can be a part of the festivities. She really did bust her buns to make it here, Sawyer, but there was bad weather, and it kept her away."

Sawyer believed it. But a part of him wanted to ask, *And Dad? Would he have tried just as hard if he'd been invited?*

Hell, it was no shock that James Marshall Fortune hadn't defied everyone for something as insignificant as his youngest and most disappointing son's birthday.

"Really, you all," Sawyer said, wearing that same smile. "It's fine."

"Sawyer…" Wyatt began.

But someone made a shushing sound, and his family turned around, looking toward the entrance.

They parted just enough for Sawyer to see what had drawn their attention.

Laurel.

She was standing there holding a small gift-wrapped box, her blond hair cascading over one shoulder. Then he took in what she was wearing—a dark blue, wispy, one-shouldered dress that came to just above her knees, with strappy silver pumps and beaded accessories.

It felt as if the oxygen had been crushed out of him. A lady. A beautiful vision.

Then again, she'd be breathtaking whether she was in jeans or a flight suit or a dress. Cocktail attire didn't make her any different from the Laurel who didn't wear makeup and liked to drink soda at bars.

He would have her any way she came.

But just as a smile was overtaking him, he realized that she'd probably been standing there in time to overhear all the talk about Mom and Dad not showing up.

As usual, Sawyer pushed the embarrassment down deep, where she would never see it.

Where it would only have to come out when he knew that no one else was looking.

Laurel was perfectly aware that Sawyer and his entire family were staring at her as if she was a made-over Cinderella who'd entered the ball. And part of her was flooded with the joy of seeing him again.

Seeing him looking at her as if she was the most desirable woman in the world.

But that wasn't a new thing from Sawyer. He seemed to yearn for her when she was wearing plain clothes, too.

It was definitely a happy moment...except for the part where she'd heard everything they'd been saying about his parents not being here.

He'd seemed especially stiff at the news of his dad's absence, raising his chin, even though he'd been smiling.

But as he walked that confident walk past his family and toward her, her heart tumbled, and she forgot about everything except this moment. It was best that way, anyway, because his personal business wasn't her business.

But still...

"You made it," Sawyer said while, behind him, every partygoer checked her out.

Years of wanting to blend in made her tug at her dress with her free hand, until she caught on to what she was doing.

His family seemed to realize that they were gawking, and they began to chat with each other. Thank God.

"I was unfairly persuaded to attend," she said once

Sawyer was standing next to her. She wanted to lighten up the gray mood that had hovered over the room a minute ago. "See, a package arrived this morning, and it had this dress in it, among other things."

"All courtesy of Jasmine."

His gaze was so direct, so hot, that she could barely think straight.

She tilted her head. "So you were making arrangements with her to shop for me when I left you two alone."

"What, did you think I was sweeping her off her feet instead? Ye of little faith."

Was he waiting for her to specifically mention the sauciest item that'd been in the package? Something sheer and incredibly revealing?

She decided to let him stew about the bodysuit. Instead, she held out the gift box she'd wrapped that morning. "Happy birthday, Sawyer."

As he took it from her, his mouth lifted at the corners, only slightly, as if he hadn't expected her to bring him anything.

She said, "It's the least I can do with what you've already given me. And thank you for all of it, by the way."

"You're more than welcome."

He shook the gift, and it reminded her of what Tanner and Parker used to do during birthdays and Christmases when they'd barely been able to eke out presents for one another because her family had been so broke.

"It's not much," she said. "I knew I should get you something that you wanted rather than needed, right? What else could I get a Fortune?"

His answering look nearly floored her: raw desire. A wanting that collided with need, creating sparks.

I'd take you *gift-wrapped,* that look said.

She searched for something to remark on, ending up with, "It's just a certificate for those flying lessons."

He reached out and took her fingers in his. "Thank you, Laur."

Why did it sound as if she'd gotten him the only thing he'd ever wanted? Was he so charming that he could make any girl believe what he wanted her to?

Yes, and she needed to remember that.

"Come on," he said, pulling her toward his family. "Be a party person. Mingle."

But it seemed as if there were other Fortunes who'd gotten the same idea even before Sawyer had.

Shane, the oldest brother, had already ambled over, intercepting them.

He introduced himself, although there wasn't much of a need for it. Laurel had seen this dark-haired, blue-eyed Fortune all over the papers, just like the others. And what do you know, *every* Fortune guy was a hunk.

No one more than Sawyer, though, she thought, falling into small talk with Shane as Sawyer opened her present and sent her another thank-you grin.

For the rest of the night, she did mingle. And she laughed more than she thought she would, especially at Victoria's liveliness and Asher's stories about his young, spirited son, Jace.

By the time everyone started to filter out of the gazebo, Laurel wondered why she'd ever been reluctant about coming here. Fortunes didn't bite.

Sawyer escorted her outside, where night had fallen over the expanse of grass, leaving a sparkle of stars over the sky.

"I'm assuming you drove," he said, "even though I offered to send a driver for you."

"Thanks for the gesture, but I didn't see a reason to be chauffeured around. Remember—I don't drink before I fly the next day."

"Which one is yours?"

She gestured toward her old green pickup, and before he could comment on her rolling bundle of paint and wheels, she said, "It gets me where I'm going."

"I wasn't about to degrade it. It's got character."

"And a broken heater. Luckily, it's not winter yet."

"Hey, if you need to keep warm, you know where to come."

She was already all warmed up.

But she doubted they'd be hanging around together when winter arrived. She didn't say it, though, because he'd taken her hands in his, running his thumbs over her skin.

By now, everyone else had departed, leaving only the catering crew to tidy up. But their presence didn't seem to offer a girl much protection, especially when *she* was the one who wanted to jump Sawyer.

"As much as I'd love to send you home with another kiss," he said teasingly, "I'd probably better not."

What? Why? She hid her disappointment. "Who said I wanted you to kiss me, anyway?"

He chuckled, and she did, too. Like she could get away with those kinds of comebacks after last night's earth-moving lip-lock.

He turned serious. "I need to be up early and clear-headed tomorrow. My dad's coming back into town to tell all of us why he's been sneaking around and keeping secrets from the family. The closer I get to the break of dawn, the more I dread what I'll be hearing from him."

"You don't seem all that stressed out." She squeezed his hands, smiling up at him. "You handle pressure well."

"So I've heard."

His smile didn't come as naturally as it usually did.

Was she seeing the man behind the facade? The real Sawyer?

She found herself sliding her hands around his waist, hugging him.

At first he seemed surprised, but no more than she was. Laurel Redmond wasn't a hugger.

Except for now, when it felt so right.

After a pause, he put his arms around her, too, drawing her even closer, and she leaned her head against his chest.

They didn't talk as, around them, the clatter of silverware and glass sounded from the cleanup crew.

He fit her just right, didn't he? And not only in a physical way. They really were two of a kind, slow to show their true emotions, hanging out with another person as long as it was convenient.

But it was starting to feel less and less convenient as Laurel's heart fizzed with an emotion she'd never thought she would encounter again.

Remember, a little voice in her said. *Think of how it felt to be in a couple with Steve. Think of the day he made you single in the most jarring way possible.*

She pulled away from Sawyer, smoothing down her dress, then her hair.

What had she been thinking, getting all intimate like that?

"All right," he said, laughing a little, as if he'd had wayward thoughts scrambling through his mind, too.

But, then again, maybe he hadn't. Maybe he was just living in the moment, as only a Fortune had the luxury of doing.

"I should go," she said, jamming a thumb toward her pickup before she could guess what he was about any further.

"I'll cash in those flying lessons soon," he said as a farewell.

"You do that. Good luck tomorrow."

"Thanks. And happy birthday, Laur...a day early."

She lifted a hand in good-night, then walked to her pickup.

She didn't mean to glance over her shoulder at him. And she very well shouldn't have, because the sight of him standing there, watching her go, his hands in his pockets, tugged at her so hard that she almost ran to him.

But she was a woman with plans, and she miraculously stuck to this one, getting into that truck and, with a slow breath of relief, driving away.

Somehow Sawyer got through the night and made it to the morning.

Once again, sleep had been elusive, and not only because that sharp longing for Laurel wouldn't go away.

Today was the meeting with Dad.

After Sawyer got ready, then sent Laurel a quick birthday wishes text, he checked for any messages that had come in on his phone.

But there was only one, and he must've missed it during the night. It was from Dad.

"Happy birthday, son," it said. "I wish circumstances had allowed me to say that sooner, and in person, but you'll understand why I couldn't when we see each other."

Sawyer had cut off the voice mail. Dammit, how could he completely turn against his father when he made it sound as if there was good reason for everything he'd been doing?

His phone dinged, and it was Laurel, sending a text.

Go get 'em, it said with a smiley face.

For a minute, he smiled, too, until he had to get serious.

But why was something inside telling him that maybe serious was starting to apply more than it should to Laurel, as well?

He pushed the thoughts away while driving with Shane to the Double Crown Ranch, which William Fortune had offered up as neutral ground for the gathering. A distant cousin of James and his brother, John Michael, old William was a natural conciliator. It helped, too, that he hadn't gotten to know the Atlanta Fortunes until they were adults, so he came into this situation with a pretty clean slate. But now that everyone had settled in Red Rock, William had taken on the mantle of patriarch that had once been held by his cousin, the late Ryan Fortune.

After Sawyer parked the convertible, he and Shane walked through the entranceway, a veritable garden of purple sage plants, roses and flowering vines. And when they got to the door, Shane grabbed Sawyer's sleeve.

"If I start to lose my temper..." he said.

Sawyer merely nodded to him, trying to be the easygoing brother now more than ever. Then he rang the doorbell.

William himself answered, right along with his wife, Lily. He was tall, in his seventies, his blond hair iced with silver. Lily, who in her mid-sixties was still as beautiful as ever, looked at them with her exotically shaped dark eyes, smiling in a soft greeting.

They were the solid presence everyone would need.

"Good to see you two," Lily said, stepping forward to show them in. After she hugged them, she added, "You'll be meeting in the study."

William took it from there, ushering them through the house.

"Just make yourselves comfortable," he said as he left them in the room with its high-beamed ceiling and fireplace.

Sawyer took in all the details: large leather couches and sitting chairs, Western-style antiques...

Someone rose from a chair, smiling, holding her arms out.

"Happy belated birthday, Sawyer," his mother said.

Happiness burst in his chest, and he went to her, enveloping her in a bear hug.

Shane came over, too, and they included him in their embrace.

Their mother's voice was muffled. "Let a woman breathe, you two."

But she was just as joyful as they were.

After she adjusted her suit jacket, she smiled wistfully, then touched Sawyer's arm. "I'm so sorry I couldn't make it yesterday."

During the cocktail party, when Victoria had rustled

Mom up on the phone to join in on "Happy Birthday," she'd apologized then, too.

"You've already said enough sorries," Sawyer said. "And I appreciate how hard you tried to be there, Mom. The sound of your voice on that phone was gift enough."

Clara Fortune shrugged in her pink Chanel suit. "But you liked what your dad and I got you, right? I remembered how you used to collect rare coins when you were younger. We thought maybe you could take it up again."

More toys he'd left behind, just like the jet in the Atlanta hangar. Yet her gift had touched him, bringing back good memories.

Still, he wasn't sure just how much thought his dad had put into the present, and that tarnished it slightly.

"I told you, Mom," he said wholeheartedly. "I love your gift. Thank you."

She pinched his cheek, and Sawyer blushed, especially when Shane lifted a brow at him, as if completely amused by watching a grown man be reduced to a kid by his mom's affection.

Unfortunately, the lightheartedness was short-lived.

A familiar and not all that welcome voice sounded from the entry, making them turn toward it.

"Everyone's here, it seems," said James Marshall Fortune as he strolled into the room, as polished in his Armani suit as one of the charity plaques he kept on his office bookshelves.

Sawyer's posture went ramrod straight. He saw that Victoria was behind Dad, along with Garrett, Wyatt and Asher.

And none of them appeared ready to sing another round of "Happy Birthday," either.

Chapter Six

As Sawyer's father looked around at everyone in the room, he used his commanding gaze to remind them that he was a president, CEO and their parent all wrapped into one.

But just as the brothers had done on the day they'd confronted James Marshall Fortune about giving half of JMF's majority shares away to a mysterious woman, they all stared right back at him, unflinching. And this time Victoria was there to join in.

She was the one who spoke first. "I think we all need to sit down."

Her husband made his way to a couch and she took a position next to him, perching on the edge of a cushion. It was obvious that she'd brought mellow, good-humored Garrett along for moral support.

When Shane, Asher and Wyatt stayed standing, Sawyer shot them a loaded glance.

Come on, just go with it. Let Dad explain and then we can stand up to him again.

Shane paused, but then gritted his jaw, nudging Asher and Wyatt over to a bigger couch next to the chair that their mother had already claimed. She was calmly watching her husband, her hands folded in her lap.

The tick-tock of a clock on the fireplace mantel pounded in Sawyer's head. He hated being here. Hated that they were all at loggerheads.

Now, as James surveyed his family again, Sawyer could swear that there was a hint of remorse in his gaze.

For what? Keeping them all in the dark? Alienating every single one of his kids?

Wyatt led the charge. "Whatever story you have to tell, there's no excuse for how long you've kept us hanging."

"That's the truth," Shane said, hunched over, his arms resting on his thighs. His gaze was lowered as he leveled it at their dad. "If it hadn't been for my own detective work, we still wouldn't know that Jeanne Marie Fortune even existed."

"Why, Daddy?" Victoria asked, shaking her head. She was holding hands with Garrett, her voice thick.

At their younger sister's show of emotion, Shane, Asher and Wyatt all raised their voices, demanding answers of their father at once.

Sawyer was tempted to join them, but he took one look at Mom, who seemed as if her heart was breaking at the sight of her divided family, and he whistled.

The piercing sound brought immediate silence.

"We need to hear this out," he said, connecting gazes

with Shane, who closed his eyes, as if knowing that Sawyer was right. Despising that he was right.

When Dad sent Sawyer a subdued yet clearly grateful nod, bewilderment seized him. Had that just been a sign of...respect? Of thanks?

He wasn't sure. All he knew was that he'd always been a sucker for an underdog, rightly or wrongly, and if Dad was going to speak, he needed to get out from under the Fortune dog pile.

A layer of tension pressed down on the room, and Dad's voice barely sliced through it. "I spent the past few days thinking of how I'd even start to tell you all this story. No beginning seems to be the right beginning."

Wyatt huffed. "Start *somewhere*."

All the siblings gave him a silencing glance, and he sat back on the sofa, crossing his arms over his chest.

"You're right, Wyatt," Dad said. "I just need to come right out and get this over with. And it's best if you hear it from the *very* beginning."

He unbuttoned his suit jacket, and Sawyer was so unused to seeing him in any state of dishabille that it threw him off guard.

"In fact," Dad said, "I'm just going to start with my father. You didn't know Jonathan Martin Fortune, and maybe when I explain him to you, you'll understand where I'm coming from." He took a breath, then started again. "I know you kids think I'm one cold, wealthy man, but..."

He trailed off, as if he'd recently realized how he appeared to his children and hadn't liked the epiphany one bit.

Mom helped him out in a soft voice. "Just tell them

about your own detective work and your P.I.s." She addressed her children. "James found out quite a bit about the family, including that his father was as cold as they came. Wasn't he, James?"

He smiled at his wife, and for the first time in Sawyer's life, he saw them as a true team.

When had that happened?

Then Dad's voice went flat. "It turns out my father never wanted children. Back in 1950, when my mother gave birth to their first child—your uncle John Michael—my father barely tolerated his presence. Then she got pregnant again, and he was furious."

Victoria asked, "He was angry at Grandma Rebecca for something he had a part in?"

"Yes." James had tugged loose his tie, and it made him seem even more human, less like the iron businessman he'd always been. "He wanted her to terminate the pregnancy. You should know that he wasn't abusive, but when he found out that she was carrying more than one child, that pushed him over the edge."

If the room had been silent before, it was silent times a thousand now. It was obvious that Dad was talking about how Grandma had gotten pregnant with him and Jeanne Marie.

Dad continued. "After Jeanne Marie and I were born, Mother was hopeful that my father would come to love us. But things got progressively worse. My father felt that she favored the children over him and seemed to have no understanding of how difficult it was raising so many kids. So one night she decided to get away from him. She packed us up and left."

Victoria was looking at her husband as if he were

her rock, but Shane, Asher and Wyatt were as stock-still as Sawyer.

So far this story wasn't exactly a family fairy tale.

"Even though Mom tried hard to make it on her own," Dad said, "it was impossible to find work with so many little babies. I found out that she ended up having to place us in foster care until a family came forward, offering to adopt…"

His voice broke off, and this time, Sawyer stepped in.

"Jeanne Marie?" he asked.

"Yes," Dad said. "They wanted Jeanne Marie. It broke Mother's heart to have to do it, but she relinquished her rights, hoping to give her a shot at a better life. She prayed that Jeanne Marie would be too young to remember she had a family before her new one. The O'Learys."

"So…" Victoria said, frowning. "We never knew about Jeanne Marie because she was adopted out of the family. Why didn't anyone tell us all of this before now?"

"I'm getting to that part," Dad said, his shoulders slumped. He looked truly tired, and Sawyer still couldn't reconcile the sight with the father he'd always known.

Dad sighed. "Eventually, Mother got back on her feet and was able to reclaim us boys, at least. John was four and I was two by then. I don't think John remembered that we had a sister, and I sure didn't, but I do recall wondering why our mother would sit by the window with a mournful look on her face every day. Eventually I found out that she thought it'd be confusing to uproot Jeanne Marie from a happy, loving home."

Sawyer asked, "And what about your dad?" He didn't call him *Grandpa*. "You must've wondered why you didn't have a father around the house."

"Your grandmother would simply tell us that 'Daddy had to go away.' If we questioned that, she wouldn't say any more.

"Anyway, he died of a heart attack a few years later, never having made up with anyone in our family. And because he and Mother had never officially divorced, she inherited the bulk of his estate. We went from poverty to poshness in the space of a week."

Was it possible that, even though James had been so very young, something had stuck with him about being poor, and he'd decided to never be that way in the future? No wonder he was such a frosty tycoon.

"But," he added, "when we moved back into the Fortune mansion, we never talked about those early years again. Mother never, ever mentioned Jeanne Marie in particular. I think Mother believed we'd love her less if we found out she 'didn't want' the other child, and she thought it would also be heartbreaking for me and John to know that our sister was with another family."

Dad was smiling to himself now, and Sawyer wasn't sure why.

"Even if I didn't remember having a twin," he said quietly, "I would get a feeling every once in a while that something was missing. That I was somehow…incomplete. I wasn't ever able to shake it, either." Then his smile faded. "But anytime I asked my brother about it, John would tell me that I was imagining things."

Wyatt had taken his hand away from his mouth. "What triggered all these…feelings?"

Dad sat on the arm of the chair his wife was in. She put her hand on his arm, smiling up at him. He seemed to take strength from that. "After your grandma's death,

I found some items among her possessions that were… odd. Two little pink baby blankets and a couple of small stuffed animals. That's what triggered a memory—but I wasn't sure what it was, exactly. Yet it was enough to tell me that these items were significant. So I started a search that very day to find out why those items had a hold on me and wouldn't let go. I hired a P.I., but I was active in the investigation myself, too. It took years to track down Jeanne Marie, mostly because her adoption records were closed, and I had no idea where she'd gone or what her last name was."

Sawyer asked, "Did Uncle John help you out?"

Dad's laugh was short. "When I shared my suspicions with him, he told me that it was all just wishful thinking on my part. He said *he* didn't remember another baby."

Shane narrowed his gaze. "This is why you two had that falling-out years ago?"

"I'm afraid so. I was adamant about my suspicions— you could even say they were haunting me. He thought I'd gone over the edge, and I got resentful about that, accusing him of being as cold as the P.I. had told me our father was. Then there was the matter of the P.I. discovering other details about our parents' marriage that John didn't want to hear, as well."

Like the way Grandma Rebecca had been emotionally beaten down enough to have left the house with her children…the verbal nastiness…

Victoria asked, "When exactly did you find Jeanne Marie?"

"Last December." Dad seemed relieved that his kids were asking questions instead of hurling accusations. "I told John about tracking her down, and he only cau-

tioned me about falling prey to a con artist. But you kids
have met her, so you have to know that's not true. She's
a good woman."

Dad laughed without mirth, shaking his head. Sawyer didn't understand Uncle John's unwillingness to at
least explore who Jeanne Marie was, either.

"But *you* tracked *her* down," Sawyer said. "She didn't
introduce herself into your life."

"Yes, and John knew that, but he thought she would
take advantage of me and my 'soft heart,' as he called it.
I didn't listen, though, and I went to see Jeanne Marie
for myself."

Another smile lit over Dad's face as he linked gazes
with Mom. It was heartening to see them looking at each
other like this during a time when many other couples
might be cracking under the pressure.

This is what it's like to have a real partner, Sawyer
thought. *A mental twin. Someone who understands you.*

Like Laurel seemed to do with him?

His dad started up again before Sawyer could think
on that too much.

"Once I met Jeanne Marie," he said, "I knew she was
definitely my twin. I didn't need a DNA test to confirm
anything, although she would've willingly gone along.
She didn't know anything about her birth family and
was overjoyed that she didn't just have one brother, but
two. Yet as I sat there in her run-down home, I felt ill.
She'd lived her whole life in relative poverty while John
and I were millionaires, raised with money. It didn't
seem fair."

Shane let out a jagged laugh as he stood from the sofa,
running his hand through his dark hair as he turned his

back on James and then came to face him. "That's why you gave her half of JMF's majority shares, isn't it?"

Wyatt joined in, sitting forward on the couch. "You felt that Jeanne Marie rightfully deserved money from your father's estate? That's why you went ahead and made such a rash move without consulting anyone?"

Mom's chin had gone up a notch, as if she were chomping at the bit to defend Dad. Obviously, she knew that there had to be more to the story, and all Sawyer wanted to do was hear it.

He said, "Uncle John still believes Jeanne Marie is a fake looking to cash in on the family name, doesn't he? And he thinks you're more of a fool than ever."

"I'm afraid so," Dad said, wiping a hand down his face.

Sawyer met his siblings' gazes, one by one. They were just as astonished as he was to see their typically cold, removed father so emotionally involved. For God's sake—he'd even willingly parted with the company's money, even without confirmation of Jeanne Marie's parentage.

Uncle John's behavior was closer to what Sawyer—and no doubt the others—would've expected of their father, who was looking around the room at his family again. But unlike earlier, he was a different man. There was none of the arrogance or defensiveness he'd exhibited when he'd first sauntered in here. There was only a disheveled guy who'd loosened his suit—his armor—piece by piece, exposing a vulnerability that Sawyer couldn't grasp.

Was he about to ask for their forgiveness?

Would they give it to him?

Would *he?*

On the smaller couch, Garrett was whispering into Victoria's ear. She nodded.

Even though he'd remained silent this entire time, Garrett talked now. "Anyone need a drink? I'm making a run to the kitchen."

Garrett wasn't a fool—he knew they were down to core-family time now. He wasn't here to forgive or not forgive James like the rest of them.

No one took him up on the offer.

As soon as Garrett left the room, Dad said, "I know I haven't been a great father, and I'm sorry. I could tell you that I suspect my coldness goes back to my childhood, with a cruel father who must've provided a terrible example of how a man should act, even if I was too young to really remember details. Or that my time in foster care affected me. I don't know if any of that would be excuse enough. And if I added that spending time away from my twin only gave me more of an isolated feeling…"

Victoria took up where he'd left off. "You had scars. You knew they were there, even if you didn't know why. Is that what you're trying to say?"

His mouth was a firm line, as if he was holding back more emotion. Sawyer glanced away, not knowing if his father wanted their sympathy.

He guessed he'd grown up watching his own dad's behavior and learning from it, too. Neither of them were big fans of pity.

Finally, James was able to talk, especially after Clara took him by the hand and raised it to her cheek, supporting him, her eyes shiny.

He dragged his gaze away from her. "I can't ask you to feel anything for me that I don't deserve, but I'm begging all of you to get to know your aunt better and not to judge her before you do. None of this is Jeanne Marie's fault, and your uncle John is absolutely wrong about her. She's not a…"

"Gold digger," Sawyer said before anyone else could.

Shane shifted on his feet. He knew Sawyer was including his fiancée, Lia, in that comment because they'd all recently judged *her* before they knew better.

His brother darted a sharp look to him, but Sawyer didn't even blink. In fact, all his siblings were giving him glances that said maybe he was being *too* easygoing with Dad.

They just hadn't forgiven their father yet, and they were going to make him work even harder for it. But something needful in Sawyer was ready to let bygones be bygones—something inside a son who'd never been loved the way he thought his siblings had been loved. Plus, he felt bad for Jeanne Marie, who was an outsider, too.

"I'd like to sit down with Jeanne Marie again," Sawyer said, hoping everyone else would follow his lead.

No dice.

But James sent Sawyer a grateful glance. Was he finally valuing Sawyer's open attitude? Was this all it took—a crisis that had put Dad into a different position so he could reevaluate his family?

Even though Dad had come clean, Sawyer still sensed the tension lingering, like electrified air that was about to give way to another storm if someone said the wrong thing.

Someone did.

Only now did Sawyer realize that Asher, who'd been so reflective during the discussion, had actually been fuming.

"I understand that there're some heavy family issues at stake," he said. "But we need to discuss why Dad gave away half of JMF Financial to a woman he might not even be related to. That was pretty extreme, and I can't help thinking that it requires more input from us."

That's when the hardest questions came out from the Fortune children, wounded and confused: *No one has worked as hard as we have for a stake in the company... We started out with money, sure, but we built what we had up even greater heights...*

And most of all, *What if Jeanne Marie really is an opportunist?*

Dad tried to raise his voice above everyone else's. "Wait! I have a lot more to tell you—"

Just as Sawyer was about to ask what he was talking about, Asher cut him off.

"The bottom line is that you should have told us everything as soon as you knew, Dad. You may say you value family, but what about us? Your kids? Where else have you been all these months and why have you been stonewalling us? You couldn't have been spending that much time just on Jeanne Marie."

As everyone but Sawyer agreed, Dad lowered his head.

Until Clara stood up from her chair, her tone firm.

"Listen!"

When their mother asked them to do something, they did it. There wasn't a peep now.

"You all need to trust your father. He really does have everyone's best interests at heart."

Much to Sawyer's shock, William Fortune interrupted from the entry. Had he been staying close in case they needed a referee?

"That should about do it for the afternoon, then," the older man said, wandering into their midst, his voice level. "I'm calling a recess. Maybe y'all need some time apart to mull over this situation."

Shane started to speak. "Now, William—"

"I mean it." The blond-and-gray man motioned toward the room's exit. "I recommend that you part ways and sort through your thoughts alone before coming together again."

No one argued with William, and everyone deserted the study.

But when Sawyer began to leave, his father kept him back.

Once again, Sawyer didn't quite recognize this man with the rumpled clothes, and his heart thudded once before seemingly going still.

"Sawyer," he said, his voice a weak imitation of what it'd been earlier, "I wanted to tell you how much your support means."

Approval. A little bit of it was all Sawyer had ever wanted, and he couldn't help but to let it show with a wary nod.

Then he said, "They're just angry, Dad. You kept everyone at bay for so long that there was plenty of time for frustration to grow."

"Not in you, though."

"Well…" Sawyer smiled without humor. "Maybe

there was some in me." Should he say it? Yeah, why not? "There's been some for a while."

Dad didn't say anything at first, but he didn't seem surprised, either. He looked at Sawyer—really seemed to look this time.

"I never thought you cared about rising through the ranks at JMF Financial," he finally said. "Maybe you think I didn't care about *you,* but I did, son. I tried to push you, just like the others, yet I felt a certain lack of interest in you. But there's something about you now, Sawyer. I don't know what it is, but I like it. And I'm happy for it."

This was the closest his father would probably come to being impressed with Sawyer, at least for now. But the thing was, Sawyer wasn't sure his life depended on getting that approval from Dad these days. Sure, it'd be nice, but…

But something had happened between Atlanta and now. Something that smelled like clean shampoo and flew the blue skies and looked impressed with him even if he hadn't tried so hard with her.

Taken aback by this realization, Sawyer stuck his hands in his trouser pockets. Dad seemed to misinterpret his body language.

"I know you probably didn't want me at your birthday yesterday," Dad said. "But that doesn't mean I wasn't thinking about you, Sawyer. Did you like the coins?"

Sawyer had almost expected Dad not to know what Mom had purchased for him. "You were definitely in on that?"

Dad actually winced. "Of course I was."

"Then yeah, Dad." He smiled. He was going to take a

Send For
2 FREE BOOKS
Today!

I accept your offer!

Please send me two free
Harlequin® Special Edition
novels and two mystery gifts
(gifts worth about $10).
I understand that these books
are completely free—even
the shipping and handling will
be paid—and I am under no
obligation to purchase anything, ever,
as explained on the back of this card.

235/335 HDL FVNA

Please Print

FIRST NAME

LAST NAME

ADDRESS

APT.#   CITY

STATE/PROV.   ZIP/POSTAL CODE

Visit us online at
www.ReaderService.com

NO POSTAGE
NECESSARY
IF MAILED
IN THE
UNITED STATES

BUSINESS REPLY MAIL
FIRST-CLASS MAIL PERMIT NO. 717 BUFFALO, NY

POSTAGE WILL BE PAID BY ADDRESSEE

HARLEQUIN READER SERVICE
PO BOX 1867
BUFFALO NY 14240-9952

new look at those coins, even if he'd thought they were valuable before. "I like them a lot."

In his dad's returned smile, as tentative as it was, Sawyer could see a new day before them. A road that'd just opened up, much like the one to Red Rock had done for him.

And much like the one that he itched to take to the airport.

Why he wanted to go there to see Laurel, he wasn't sure, exactly. Nevertheless, he forgot about asking Dad what else he'd wanted to tell them regarding Jeanne Marie and went to his car, speeding it toward the airport.

Thank God Laurel had finished work for the day. She'd just been counting out what she thought were her last minutes on earth with a wild-hearted divorcee who'd decided to buy herself flying lessons to celebrate signing the papers that would end her marriage.

And oh, boy. There'd definitely be no more merry divorcées in Laurel's cockpit, she'd decided after assuming the controls from the woman, who'd wanted to try "all those tricks that the Blue Angels do" before she was even remotely ready.

She was taking the edge off in the airport terminal's lobby, sitting near the snack bar and downing a root beer now, mulling over going home or…

Doing what? Calling Sawyer to see how his heavy-duty day had gone? Asking him to stop over so that she wouldn't be alone on her birthday?

She gulped down the soda. Yeah, she was feeling mildly sorry for herself right now, but she'd elected to work on her birthday before. Why was this time any different?

Was she in a bummer mood because she missed Sawyer, and she hated to admit it?

As if her thoughts had conjured him, he walked into the snack bar area, looking around for…her?

Her heart blasted, and she forced it to behave.

It's just lust, she told herself. *That's it.*

When he spotted her, then walked toward her, she saw that something had affected him greatly, and she knew it had to do with that meeting with his dad.

She stood. "You okay?"

"Yeah."

He came to within a couple feet of her, wearing the confident smile that always lit her up. But when she cocked her head, doubting his too-casual answer, he paused, then shook his head.

"To tell you the truth," he said, "I'm not sure if I'm okay or not."

Much to her shock, he began describing the drama on the Double Crown Ranch—his dad's story about finding Jeanne Marie, his siblings' reactions, then the rupture at the end.

"You should've seen him," Sawyer said. "My dad— the steeliest man on earth. But he wasn't like that in the end."

It seemed as if he was about to say more. Maybe about the troubles she suspected he'd had with his dad in general, based on what she'd heard at that party.…

Laurel didn't press him. If he wanted to tell her, he would. Besides, she probably shouldn't know the details.

Wouldn't that be out of bounds for no-strings-attached people?

"So," she said, putting them back on safe ground, "your family's back at square one with your dad? Nothing was really resolved?"

"Pretty much."

His shoulders sank, and she couldn't bear to see him like this. She wanted to see happy Sawyer, fun Sawyer.

He was reminding her all too much of the pain she'd nursed from all *her* family problems, and she just couldn't sit there and take it.

Luckily, she'd always known how to escape problems.

"Hey," she said, giving him a light punch in the arm.

He lifted his gaze to her.

She grinned. "It's a good thing I know exactly what you need right now, Sawyer Fortune."

As she grabbed his hand and led him out of the snack bar, the bewildered expression on his face made her smile.

Once again, she had his number.

Chapter Seven

She really had known what Sawyer needed.

But when Laurel had told him that she knew just what would cheer him up, then taken him by the hand and led him out of the snack bar, out of the terminal and toward the flight school building, he'd been thinking that she meant to...

Well, do something that didn't include taking him up in a plane.

She had prepped for a flight and brought him into a Cessna 172, zooming off into the sky, making him feel a little more weightless than he had on the ground.

As they'd nosed higher and higher, until the landmarks of Red Rock became specks on the ground, he'd felt the day roll right off his shoulders.

He'd heard of people who dreamed of flying. Maybe he'd read about it in a college general psychology class that he'd barely been paying attention in, but he remembered something about how the dream meant that you've risen above something, getting a different perspective on what lay below you.

Airborne, soaring, the whir of the small plane humming through him… Sawyer could've been dreaming, but he wasn't.

Laurel had been right—it'd been just what he'd needed. And every time he'd glanced over to see her wearing that headset, smiling as if the plane were an extension of herself, he'd been that much more at peace. And he'd felt that way until they'd touched down on the ground again.

Now, in her office, he was still buzzing from the experience.

He'd plopped down in a chair across from her desk, his ankle resting right above his knee, utterly relaxed.

"I don't recall ever feeling that way when I was learning to fly a plane," he said. "But then again, you're a smooth pilot, Laur. You made the craft feel like a Rolls-Royce up there."

She was leaning against a wall, one foot kicked over the other as she casually surveyed him. There was something about her…as if she was still up in the air, more at ease than he'd ever seen her.

And somehow more stimulated, judging from the sparkle in her eyes.

"Didn't you enjoy getting your pilot's license?" she asked.

"No, I did. At the time. But flying didn't stick." Back then, he'd been in the middle of watching his siblings move up the ladder of success at work while he stagnated. At that point, he hadn't been in the mood to feel good about much, except partying and forgetting himself in the pursuit of certain nocturnal activities.

"Why exactly did you take lessons back then?" she asked. "If you weren't going to use the license, I mean."

"Because it was something to do." He held up his hands. "There—I confess. I wanted to be Howard Hughes in his cool days. I wanted to have a status-symbol plane."

"You wanted to be a Fortune, flying your own plane because you could."

She didn't say it with any snarkiness—she was just stating a fact.

He grinned. "I haven't flown that plane in years. I should bring it out here so you can get ahold of it."

Laurel laughed. "I've never known anyone who talks about an aircraft as if it was a box of sweaters he left in an attic. Then again, I've never known anyone like you, Sawyer."

Had she meant the comment to be flirty?

Or was there a deeper meaning there?

When he glanced at her to see, she didn't reveal a thing. She only had a small, kittenish smile on her mouth.

The buzz from the flight, still lingering?

"Do you get like this every time?" he asked.

"How?"

"As if you've just had the best sex of your life."

One would think that she would've gotten used to his frankness by now, but she still widened her gaze at him. Then she laughed again.

"Sometimes I do," she said. "I liked having *you* up

there with me, though. You obviously loved it. And I think that it helped you to…"

Her tone had gone a little dark.

"What?"

She shook her head, waved her comment away. "I don't want to bring the room down."

He guessed at what she'd probably been about to say. "You think that my time up in the air with you cleared my head and made me forget about today's family meeting. Well, mission accomplished."

As she gauged him, he sat up. Might as well get this talk out of the way since he'd come here to relieve his soul to her in the first place. He hadn't known his purpose in wanting to see Laurel at first, but he'd figured it out quickly enough after he'd caught sight of her near the snack bar.

"I know you walked into my cocktail party last night just as some of our Fortune family drama was swirling around," he said. "You heard that my parents couldn't make it."

"I heard that your mom tried."

"Yeah. But I wasn't sure about my dad's intentions."

It looked as if she was deciding whether they should be talking about something this personal or not. But he wanted her to hear it, because if not her, then who?

The thought rattled him, but in a good way, rearranging his head just as the flight had.

"All my life," he said, "I've had to keep up with my brothers. And you can imagine what a Herculean task that was. They're perfect. So I had a lot to live up to. My dad's expectations were like a giant weight on me, so I would test him, see what I could get away with as the youngest son. When I realized that there was a hell of a lot he could tolerate because my brothers did enough to keep him proud, I started to…I don't know. 'Go with the flow' is a good way of putting it. Accept the status quo of my being the brother who was expendable."

Laurel came around her desk, closer to his chair. "Don't say things like that."

"That I'm not of much value?" He smiled. "It's okay. It's always been a thing with my dad. But outside school and the office…now, *that's* where I seemed to excel."

"Oh. You mean in a personal life. I'm sure your charm did wonders for it."

"Maybe so."

The light had come back into her eyes, the kind that told him she was still on some sort of high.

But was it because she'd been up in that plane…or because she was standing so close to him?

Or both?

He finished up what he'd started. "As far as my dad goes, there were times I felt that he devalued me because of how I avoided his expectations. It's been that way for years, but today…today something happened, even during all the ugliness of our family meeting. Today I think he saw that I can ease the way between him and my brothers and sister, that my laid-back attitude is good for something besides smooth-talking my way through his company's PR gauntlet."

Laurel was smiling down at him, and it was genuine, as if she was happy that he had finally started to figure things out for himself.

Out of some kind of pure emotion—he still didn't know what the hell it was—he raised a hand, touching the side of her khaki-covered leg, carelessly running his fingers to the back of her thigh ever so lightly.

As if caught off balance, she reached out, grabbing his shoulder. "Sawyer..."

She still had that look on her face—the contrail of exhilaration. A remaining glint in her eyes that probably matched his.

Screw all the serious conversation, he thought, tracing his fingers up the back of her leg until he got to the base of her spine, then palming her and pushing her forward so that she landed in his lap with a gasp.

He slid his other hand around her waist, then down and over the curve of her derriere. She bit her lip, looking as if she was deciding what should come next.

And what shouldn't.

But he could see the wild blue sky in her eyes, still making her fly, and before he knew it, she'd dug her fingers into his hair and bent down to kiss him.

It was hard and soft at the same time. He couldn't tell which, and he couldn't wrap his mind around the sensation well enough to puzzle it out.

Not that it mattered, because there was more to her kiss than ever before. A hint of uncontained passion.

An invitation.

When she ended it, she kept her lips against his, her hand at his nape.

"I keep thinking this is a bad idea," she said on a breath.

He slid his fingers down her thigh, then partway up again, and she put her hand on top of his.

"You might've started something that'll be tough

to stop," he said, grit in his tone. "You're the one who kissed me."

"Maybe I did."

And she kissed him again, sending him spinning like a buzz saw. She sucked on his bottom lip and disengaged from him, but still kept her mouth against his.

"Maybe," she said, "you ought to come over tonight."

He went into a fevered haze, not even thinking to ask what time she wanted him at her apartment as she slyly got up from his lap, ruffled his hair and walked out the door.

Leaving him rocking and rolling and dying for more.

Once Laurel had made quick time to her pickup, she had the presence of mind to text Sawyer.

All she typed was 7:00.

But she had no doubt it'd be enough information.

She squealed out of the parking lot and headed straight home.

Still having a couple of hours before the appointed time, she cleaned like a dervish—there were folded clothes on the sofa from where she'd been watching the Food Network that morning. And the knickknacks she'd picked up from her travels—everything from a Tower of London snow globe to a music box from Prague—were a little dusty, so she took a rag and polished them.

After the world's quickest vacuuming job and a sprint to change her sheets, she hopped in the shower, finally taking a breather.

She'd done it—invited a guy over to her place for the first time in years. It was almost as if she was primping for a first date as she blow-dried her hair until it was hanging straight down her back, put on the sangria-shaded lipstick she occasionally wore and slapped some red nail polish on her toes.

When she went to her kitchen to prepare some food for her and Sawyer, she second-guessed herself.

Would tonight be all about eating? Sitting around with cocktails and sharing intimate stories?

No. She'd gotten a couple intimate stories from Sawyer today, and she still wasn't sure that she should've been listening to them. Yes, her heart had gone out to him about his relationship with his dad, but she was so numb when it came to her own sperm donor that she'd been crossing her fingers that their conversation wouldn't extend into Redmond territory.

Tonight, she decided, wasn't about baring souls. It was about those benefits they'd talked about before. After flying with Sawyer, it'd seemed natural to arrive at this destination with him, her hormones growling, her sex drive revved and finally ready.

Pure sex, she thought. And that was all that would happen.

She stood in front of her closet and…damn, it was unlike her to vacillate about what she was going to wear on any given day.

Casual jeans and a T-shirt? A sage-green summer dress she hadn't put on since Juliet's anniversary party three years ago?

Laurel's gaze traveled to a chair by her bed, where she'd draped one of Sawyer's birthday gifts.

The charcoal bodysuit.

She went over to it, coasting her fingers over the sheer material and floral appliqués. It was delicate, beautiful, something she would never have pictured herself wearing.

On an urge she couldn't resist—she'd had a lot of those lately—she donned the bodysuit, then looked in the full-length mirror on the back of her bedroom door and held her breath as she got a load of herself.

She seemed…seductive. Yeah—this was really *her* in the mirror, embracing her sexuality as she never had before.

Seductive and full of heat.

When she heard her doorbell, she glanced at the clock, her heart in her throat.

Seven o'clock on the nose.

Where had the time gone?

Not knowing what else to do, she darted to her closet, tugged the summer dress off its hanger, pulled it over her head and sprinted barefoot over the carpet to the door.

When she opened it, her heartbeat circled in her chest.

Sawyer had showered, too, if his wet brown hair gave her any clue, and he was wearing a fresh beige Western shirt, jeans and his boots.

But he was bearing gifts again, and as he gestured to the shopping bag with red roses peeking out from the top, he grinned.

"You're out of breath, Laur."

"I ran to the door. You're a prompt one, aren't you?"

The gleam in his gaze told her that he would've gotten here a lot sooner if she'd suggested it.

She showed him in, and he glanced around her utilitarian apartment at her knickknacks, her framed photos that she'd taken of places like Ostia Antica near Rome and Japanese pagodas, her Ikea furniture. Then he went to her kitchen counter, setting down the bag and unloading it.

First, he handed her the roses. "For the birthday girl."

"Thank you."

She smelled them and went to get a vase from a cabinet, all too aware of her bare feet and red toenails. They made her feel summery and sexy, her nerves flaring with every moment that passed.

He put two bottles on the counter—chilled champagne and sparkling cider—plus a cake box.

"You didn't," she said.

"Why wouldn't I?"

He thought of everything. She couldn't say as much for herself, though.

"I didn't have time to cook, I'm afraid." Man, was she out of practice with this date stuff.

But all she'd been able to think about had been her libido. She wasn't sure he'd complain about that, though.

He was sweeping a deliberate gaze from her painted toenails, then up her legs, her waist, her chest, to her face. By the time he was done, she was red all over.

"You look beautiful," he said.

"Oh?" How did he get her to blush all the time? "This is such an old dress. I never wear it."

"You should. Actually, you should wear more dresses. You've got the legs for them."

If another guy had offered her such a blatant charm-filled line, she would've smacked him. But Sawyer could get away with just about anything with her.

Especially tonight.

He opened the cake box, and she came over to take a peek inside.

It was small but fancy, reminding her of a wedding cake. The icing had her name written over it in red gel, making her think that *Laurel* sort of looked like a stretched-out heart.

But she was seeing things.

"Sawyer, you don't have to try so hard, you know." Still, she was secretly pleased to be treated so well. She wasn't used to it.

"Maybe I shouldn't tell you this," he said, "but when I got to the bakery counter at the market, this cake was the freshest thing they had left. They frosted over the top so it would look as if it was made for you. It's all they could do at the last minute."

"It's great." She wickedly sneaked a finger full of icing from the bottom, tasting it, but he didn't seem to mind. "If this was bigger, I'd say that someone didn't pick up their wedding cake."

"You're right. This is the top layer. They gutted the thing for us." He raised a brow. "I wonder if this is an indication that there'll be a run of disastrous wedding plans for Red Rock."

"What do you mean?"

"When I got home, Shane let me know that my three brothers are still threatening to bar Dad from their wedding. This cake could be an omen."

Was he about to sink into the dumps? It didn't seem like it, but then again, it'd occurred to her before that Sawyer was pretty good at hiding his real feelings, wearing a grin instead of a frown.

With her clean hand, she laid her palm on his arm, smiling, letting him know that he shouldn't worry about a thing.

His answering smile was real—she knew enough about him by now to tell.

Her heart fluttering, she continued to lighten the mood, taking another finger full of icing, holding it up, and from the glimmer in his eyes, he was wondering what she was going to do with it.

"Your brothers should just elope," she said. "Weddings are only a bunch of trouble and overrated, anyway. And marriage…?"

He took up the teasing. "Marriage just leads to expectations that simply can't be fulfilled."

"There goes our shared mind again."

"That's what happens when you're the last two people standing after the Red Rock Plague."

They laughed, but his mirth died when she eased her finger into her mouth, sucking off the icing. She didn't look at him while she did it—she merely acted as if this was how birthday girls in summer dresses and red-painted toenails frittered away their time.

She could feel his gaze burning into her. Good.

"Know what's funny?" she asked after she'd swallowed.

Suddenly, he was busy with the champagne, unwrapping the foil from its top. "What?"

Poor guy. She might have to take it easy on him tonight.

Right.

"When I was young," she said, "I had this group of friends. They were very girly-girl. We played dolls and dressed in all our moms' clothes when they weren't home, pretending we were grown-ups. I just kind of went along with everything—I didn't want to be the weird kid on the block, especially since I was a couple grades ahead of everyone and already kind of a freak for my age. But when we got a little older, they went through a phase where they'd come up with bridal fantasies and revel in sharing them."

She went to a cabinet and brought out two flutes for the drinks, but she began to open the sparkling cider for herself since tomorrow was a flying day.

"Did *you* have a fantasy?" Sawyer asked.

"A half-baked one. I didn't put much creativity into it—the game bored me too much. Plus, I was reading *Jane Eyre* at the time, so I borrowed a description of the kind of gown she would've worn. Mr. Rochester said he would 'dress her in jewels and in finery befitting her new social station.' The girls loved that, except…well, you know me—I just had to add that Jane freaked out at Mr. Rochester's promise because she had a bad feeling about the wedding."

"I guess because, from what you saw with your mom's marriage, matrimony never works out."

Laurel swiveled their conversation around.

"Here," she said, pouring the cider into her glass. "Let's make another toast, just like we did when we said we'd avoid the Red Rock Plague."

After she grabbed the champagne and poured some for him, they lifted their flutes.

"To living in reality," she said.

He angled his head, and she didn't know what he was thinking as they clinked glasses and drank.

Had she blown them back into intimate talk by expanding on the subject of weddings?

Dammit, she wasn't going to see this night go by

without doing what she wanted to do with Sawyer, so she put down her flute and leaned on the counter, hoping he'd see what she was wearing under her dress.

When his gaze heated on a flare of passion, she knew that she'd taken the right, seductive step.

She was wearing the lingerie he'd bought her.

Sawyer's blood beat a fierce tattoo in his veins as he tried to recover.

Was she showing him the bodysuit on purpose?

Based on the look in her eyes, steamy and willing, he'd say yes.

And when she dipped her finger into the cake's frosting once again, he couldn't stop himself from imagining what it would taste like if he licked it off.

She didn't do anything with the frosting, merely crooking her finger as she tilted her head. "You didn't happen to eat before you got here," she said. "Did you?"

The last thing he'd had on his mind had been real food—just birthday cake, flowers and Laurel.

"I'm not all that hungry. For true grub, anyway."

"What are you in the mood for, then?"

She waved her icing-coated finger, and he put his elbows on the counter until they were nearly face-to-face.

"Cake sounds good," he said, his gut tightening.

"You'll like the taste of this, then," she said in a low voice.

He took that as permission to get even closer to her, his mouth less than an inch from her finger. But just as his lips nearly touched her, she pulled her hand back, easing her finger into her own mouth, eating the frosting.

"Mmm."

She was smiling, toying with him.

But he was pretty good at this type of thing himself, so he glided his own finger around the edge of the cake.

"That's right," she said. "Plenty there for you, too."

Before she could react, he reached out and swiped the icing down her nose.

Her lips parted, as if she couldn't believe he'd done that.

He laughed.

"You think that's funny?" she asked.

"I *know* that's funny. No thinking about it. You're real cute with a white streak down your nose, like a kid who fell face-first into the birthday table."

Her answer was to scoop another serving and dot it on his nose, too.

"Oops," she said. "Looks like you took a fall, too."

He was taking a fall, all right, and he feared it was for Laurel.

But oddly, that didn't scare him as much as it would've with anyone else. It was just a matter of course—an inevitability that had come crashing down on him so fast that he hadn't seen it coming.

Until now.

Relieved that he'd finally admitted it, he kept the game going, getting more frosting on his thumb and smearing it over her mouth.

This time, her laughter rang through the room as she made a dive for the whole cake.

"Oh, no, you don't," he said, lunging for her before she got to it, taking her into his arms and crushing his mouth to hers.

She sank against him, one hand raised as if she still

intended to go for the cake. But Sawyer didn't care. Frosting made the kiss sweet and messy, and he ate it off her lips, licking, fisting her hair to press her closer as she dug the nails of her free hand into his back, making a little sound in her throat.

A pleased sound.

A moan that nearly killed him.

Everything spun around Sawyer's mind, blinding him as they lost their balance, his back hitting the counter when she slanted her entire length against him, standing on her tiptoes, sucking at his lips to get the last of the frosting on *him*.

Then she was tearing at the buttons on his shirt with one hand, ripping it open. A cool breeze from her air conditioner nipped at his skin, but her body was heated, sending flames wherever she melded to him.

When she broke away from the kiss, both of them were desperate for air.

"So that's how it's gonna be," she said. "Icing on the cake…or on one of us?"

He ran a finger down her nose, getting the frosting off it and enjoying the treat.

After he wiped the icing off his nose, too, he said, "This doesn't quite make my appetite go away."

A naughty smile lit over her lips, and she ducked around him, succeeding in snatching a fistful of cake and smearing it over his chest.

"My appetite's just starting," she said.

And damn it all if she didn't press her lips against his chest, nibbling at him and the cake, crumbs falling to the floor as he leaned back against the counter.

He'd never gotten a better birthday gift, he thought, reaching for the hem of her dress.

But he hadn't unwrapped all of it yet.

Chapter Eight

The next thing Laurel knew, Sawyer had reached for the bottom of her dress and was yanking it up and over her head, tossing it to the side and leaving her in only that bodysuit.

He paused, slowing things down, his hands on her waist. He was gripping her, but not hard.

Just enough to send shivers through her.

"Dammit, Laurel," he said, almost sounding strangled.

Then he scooped her into a kiss again, the taste of sugar from the cake lingering in her mouth, mixing with the essence of him.

She swayed into him, just as weak as he always made her.

Yet this was the only way she would allow herself to lose strength when it came to Sawyer. She would give herself up to fun—fun just like *this*.

But not anything else.

He started to walk her backward, toward her bedroom, but when they didn't get anywhere—not when the kissing was keeping them so unfocused—he picked her up.

Wrapping her legs around his hips, she wiggled against him.

"I'm not gonna get you anywhere if you're doing that," he said.

But she didn't stop teasing him. Streams of heat were shooting up and through her, and she couldn't stop if she wanted to.

They made it to her room, though, and when they got to her bed, he gently laid her down, resting one hand on her stomach.

A million brutal beats gathered there, as if drawn to the shape of his hand. She ached more than she ever had for him, and that ache was reaching up, like a split of lightning, tearing her apart and grasping for her heart.

But it never quite got *there*. She wouldn't let it.

Still, there was a whole lot else she would let happen.

As Sawyer mapped the lines of her waist, traveling his hands up until he cupped her breasts, she leaned her head back, groaning.

And when he traced the undersides of her breasts through the sheer bodysuit material, she strained against his hands, feeling her nipples tightening.

What made her even more passionate was the thought that he couldn't see everything about her body yet—the appliqués on the suit were covering her nipples. Same with down below, where there was another game of peekaboo going on with similar floral designs.

"As nice as this lingerie is," he said, "I want it off."

"You'll have to earn the privilege." Saucy. He brought it out in her.

A sinful grin spread over his mouth. "And how do I earn it?"

He didn't wait for her to parry, instead slipping his thumbs up, over her nipples, circling them. Need drilled between her legs, and she bit her lip.

He said, "I like the idea of doing this slowly, watching your face, because you know what?" He leaned in close, his words bathing her ear. "I have *your* number tonight."

It sounded as if he'd gotten too far into her psyche— as if he knew more about her than anyone ever had. The notion sent her heart into a jolting shock.

No one would ever get to her.

Never again.

But her logic faded as he reached around to the back of the bodysuit, unzipping it. She closed her eyes, unable to resist—at least this.

"As I recollect," he said, "Madame Luna told me my number is thirteen. I'm gonna make a prediction here myself. I'm gonna say that's your number, too."

What was he talking about?

He peeled down the top of the bodysuit to expose just one breast and got onto the bed, his weight making the mattress dip. Then he bent to take her nipple into his mouth.

He laved it, sucked on it, and she squirmed beneath him. She was about to pop, but she didn't know exactly where. It felt as if a hundred explosions were competing to be the first to break inside her.

After he came up for air, he smiled at her. "That was one kiss."

"You'll have to do a lot more earning."

"I'm working on it."

She already knew where kiss number two would be. And as he drew down the other side of the bodysuit to reveal her other breast, she turned her head aside, restless and needful.

He paid as much attention to this breast as the first, and when he was done, dragging down her bodysuit until it bunched around her hips, she had no clue where number three would be.

Surprising her, he turned her over, coasting his hands up her bare back, then down.

Just as she started to hold her breath, he gave her a third number, nipping the skin at the small of her back.

She gasped, arching away from the bed as he traced his mouth up her spine.

Already she'd lost count of the numbers. He could've done five thousand things to her and she would've been mired in a tangle of sixes and eights.

All she knew was that he didn't seem to miss an inch of her: lightly biting her shoulder, pushing aside her hair to kiss her nape then rub his lips against her neck.

"They say," he murmured there, against the sweet spot, "that thirteen's pretty unlucky."

That must've been where they were now.

Thirteen.

"But," he said, coaxing his hand down between her legs, "I don't believe in bad luck."

She buried her face in the mattress just as he stroked her once again, kissing her neck at the same time.

Her head was a bundle of equations that made no sense. All her learning flew away like a flapping crash of wings, leaving something new to rise and take its place.

Clutching at the bedspread, she moaned with every caress, her voice getting higher and higher, sharp edges pushing against her until she knew that she was going to burst all over.

He seemed to be an expert on just when to leave her hanging, because he turned her over just then, pulling the bodysuit off her in one fluid movement.

Unleashed, she sat up, tearing his shirt off all the way, helping him to fumble off his jeans and boots and all the rest.

But it seemed that he didn't think the number thirteen was enough for them, and after he snatched a condom from a pocket of his discarded jeans, he guided her back down to the bed.

He lowered himself to her thighs, kissing them on the inside, working his way up as she lifted her hips to meet him.

"Laurel," he said against her skin, just before he hit home, kissing her between the legs.

A slam of desire got her right away, making her fly in all directions, making her cry out at the fierce explosion.

He kissed there again and again, taking his time, building her up until she couldn't stand it anymore and she pulled at his hair, urging him upward so he could press his mouth against hers.

As their lips met, she felt as if she'd been exposed in every way.

But how?

And why?

She'd never planned for this to happen....

He kept his body against hers as he took the condom out of the packaging, then slid it over himself. Finally, he kissed her once more, then paused to look into her eyes while pushing the sweat-dampened hair back from her face.

There was something there, in his gaze. Something she'd noticed before but had wanted to ignore or explain away.

Did he see it in her, too?

No, he couldn't. Because there *wasn't* any kind of growing attachment in her.

"Let's do this," she whispered, taking him by the hips, wiggling beneath him once again.

It was obviously too much for him, and he groaned, entering her.

She made a surprised sound. It'd been so long, and he filled her up so well....

And it wasn't just in a physical way, either. She felt full in her heart, and she didn't know why, because she'd been working so hard to protect against it.

But as they moved together, all those shields around her melted, slipping, gathering into a molten pool in her belly.

And that pool was spreading, simmering...

Bubbling...

Popping once again until it pressed out against her, pushing, pushing—

Another slam, another wave that decimated her. She heard herself say his name over and over, heard him groan again as he came to his own climax soon afterward.

As they collected themselves, she stroked his hair,

kept him close, not knowing how much longer she'd allow herself to be this vulnerable.

Maybe for a while, she thought as he kissed the sweet spot on her neck again.

Maybe just until morning came and they could go back to normal.

Sawyer woke in a bed that wasn't his.

And all by himself.

As the events of the night before came back to him, he smiled, hearing the sound of Laurel in her kitchen outside of the open door. He smelled roasted coffee and muffins.

Most of all, though, he smelled her clean shampoo on the sheets, and he stayed in bed a few minutes longer, taking in her essence.

She'd brought him to a place he'd never expected last night. A few times, too.

After the first time, it hadn't taken long for him to recover, and they'd gone for an encore. Then there'd been the shower. Then they hadn't even made it back to the bed.

Every time, Sawyer's heart had rotated to a different position in his chest. Or at least it felt like it. He wasn't sure if it'd just gone off-kilter, or if it'd finally settled in a spot that it'd been meant to occupy all along.

Either way, last night had changed everything for him, even if he couldn't define what everything was just yet.

But what about Laurel?

He wasn't sure, because whenever he'd found himself looking deep into her gaze, she'd given him a flirty smile or initiated another round of sex, as if that's all she wanted from him.

Then again, Laurel could be hard to read. Plus, he couldn't expect a woman who'd been treated as she had been by an absentee father and a jerk boyfriend to warm up to intimacy right away.

Maybe it'd just take some time for her to get used to what he was starting to feel....

Sawyer sat up in the bed, ruffling his hair. Good thing he had all the time in the world to see if these new feelings would stick with *him*.

After pulling himself together in the bathroom, he found his jeans on the floor and donned them, then made his way out to the kitchen, pushing his hair away from his face and probably making it even messier.

"Morning," she said casually, already sitting at the table fully dressed in her khakis and a polo shirt with the Redmond Flight School logo on the front. She was drinking a cup of coffee with a plate of minimuffins and berries on the side.

Her smile was just as it always was—light and appealing, but...

But was there something else about her? Something... off?

He nodded to her, grinning at the plate she'd made for him, too. "Morning. Looks like you got up bright and early."

"You sleep like a rock. I already took a shower and everything."

"You wore me out, that's why I slumbered through it all."

As he sat, she remained friendly yet cool, just as if

they'd met each other merely a day ago and hadn't ever talked much or eaten dinner together or had birthday cake...

A raging flush swallowed him up as he thought of last night again.

When she glanced at her watch, he got the feeling that she couldn't wait for him to be on his way.

Was he being paranoid? Usually he was the one who was in a hurry to skedaddle the morning after.

"You got somewhere to be today?" he asked. "No, let me guess. A charter flight."

"Just a couple of lessons, Fortune. I'm due in at eight o'clock to prep."

Had she really just called him by his last name?

Now he got another feeling—that maybe she'd woken up and started regretting last night, or that she'd second-guessed everything and thought she'd gone too far with him. That she wasn't about to open herself up to betrayal from a man once again.

But was he reading too much into her?

As if confirming his suspicions, she got up from the table, heading for the sink, where she tossed the rest of her coffee.

"Laurel," he said. "What's going on?"

She sent a "who, me?" glance over her shoulder, her low blond ponytail swiping her back.

"Nothing," she said.

"You seem...jumpy."

She laughed, as if it was the most ridiculous comment in the world. But when he noticed that the cake box was nowhere in sight, he also started wondering if she'd thrown it away, getting rid of all the evidence of a reckless night.

The kind of night a careful woman like Laurel didn't do.

As she cleaned up, he decided he was being overly wary and wolfed down his food. The chocolate-chip muffin was fresh, the coffee strong, as if she knew how he took it.

Then again, she could've just been expecting him to pour some sugar and cream in it, because the condiments were right there on the table.

Damn, she was driving him in all kinds of scattered directions, and it didn't sit well.

Purposefully, he went to the kitchen, carrying his plate. When he leaned over her to put it in the sink, he pressed his chest to her back.

She went stiff, but then, with a recovering smile, went about drying a mug again.

Yeah, she was off. And he wasn't buying this casual act, either.

Even though another gut feeling told him not to push Laurel to tell him what was on her mind, he certainly wasn't going to leave without reminding her of how good it'd been last night.

He eased his arms around her, and she dropped her hands, the mug banging against the counter before she let go of it.

"Klutz," he said kiddingly.

"It was still slippery," she said in a whisper.

He refrained from the temptation of using her comment for a few double entendres.

"Before I go, I just want to thank you for everything," he said, stroking a hand over her stomach.

She took in a breath, then laughed it out. "Same here. That cake, the drinks and flowers were all so thoughtful. If you want any leftovers, I put the cake in the fridge."

"Nah. Just leave some in there for me."

She laughed again, as if he'd been joking.

Had he been?

The only thing he knew for sure was that this was one skittish woman. But maybe she was smart to take everything slow.

Maybe he was moving too fast into uncharted territory with this woman.

Keeping it low-key, he kissed her below the ear, and she squeezed his hand that was still on her stomach, as if in an unthinking response.

"Have a good one," he said as he backed away from her.

"You off to ride the range?" she asked.

She'd turned around, her hands braced back on the sink.

Jeez. Did she want him to go or not? He was getting whiplash.

"I'm making arrangements to see Jeanne Marie today," he said. "Nobody knows it, though, except for you, now."

She nodded, then, as if she didn't know what to say next, gestured toward the door. "I'm going to take off, if you don't mind. Just lock the door from the inside on the knob when you leave?"

"I'll do that."

Smiling, she started to turn back toward the counter, but hesitated. Then she spoke.

"Really, Sawyer. Thank you for everything. It really was a great birthday."

As she faced the sink again, turning on the faucet, he shook his head, wondering if he'd be able to figure her out as the day wore on.

Sawyer had found out from his father that he'd invited Jeanne Marie back to Red Rock during this family crisis, and he'd put her up in La Casa Paloma Hotel, in the lap of luxury.

Normally she lived in a town called Horseback Hollow, near Lubbock, but he'd wanted her nearby, making it easy for anyone who cared to visit her to do so.

Sawyer did her the service of calling beforehand to arrange a time to meet, and she gladly invited him up to her suite right away, sounding surprised yet touched that he cared to see her at all.

When he arrived, she greeted him at her door, a tall woman his father's age, with gray hair in a tidy bun and a face that was wrinkled yet attractive in a striking way. She was wearing a simple light-blue blouse with darker pants, and if she were to take a stroll around the lush hotel property, no one would mistake her for a guest who seemed right at home.

"Sawyer," she said, and for a moment, he thought she might rush forward to embrace him.

But she knew about the strife her presence had caused the family, and she reached out a hand for him to shake instead.

Sawyer was having none of that, though. Back when

he'd met her for the first time nearly a month ago, he'd had no doubts that this woman was his dad's twin. Just one look confirmed it.

He hugged her.

She seemed as pleased as punch about that, patting him on the back and giving him a glowing smile when they pulled away from each other.

"You were brave to show up," she said. "Clara told me that your meeting yesterday left most of your siblings fit to be tied."

Sawyer should've known his mom would graciously welcome Jeanne Marie into the family in a show of support for her husband.

"Everyone's still working things out," he said, softening the blow of the truth.

As Jeanne Marie held his gaze, hers faded with sadness. "I never meant to cause such dissension in the family. I was as shocked as anyone to find out I'm related to James. I always knew I was adopted, but I had no idea that I had any birth siblings out there."

"This has to be rough on you."

"It hasn't been the best time I've ever had, I'll tell you that. But James insists that I stay here until matters are resolved. I think that means he wants every single one of you children to accept me, and he'll be happy with no less."

"He's stubborn like that."

She laughed slightly, and it reminded Sawyer of how his dad had laughed yesterday when he was hurt.

Then she waved him inside. "Come in. You're a coffee drinker, aren't you?"

"Who isn't?"

"I like my tea, and I was over the moon to see the selection they have here. But what don't they have at this place?"

Sawyer was just about to note that his father was a tea fan, too, when he saw how Jeanne Marie had laid coffee out on a table by the balcony as sunlight streamed into the room from the open window.

He smiled as he pulled a chair out for her. "You realize that there's room service here, and you can use it whenever you want."

"Oh, never mind that." She sat, poured coffee into a waiting mug for him, then some already-steeped tea from a pot into her cup. "I'd be perfectly happy with a fraction of what this room has in it."

And she didn't seem to be fibbing. She'd been taken from very modest means to this—a room with silk sheets, designer furniture and probably a whirlpool bathtub. He couldn't imagine the culture shock she was going through.

From relative poverty to poshness, he thought, remembering what his dad had said yesterday about how he and Uncle John had gotten suddenly rich after their father had died.

"So this is nice," she said. "Having my nephew visit me. It's too bad that I didn't know you when you were growing up. I would have been a wonderful aunt."

"You would've taken me to the zoo and all that stuff?"

"Yes, I would've been the fun relative." She smiled, but she was obviously referring to Uncle John, who was just as starchy as Dad. And from the way she raised her chin ever so slightly at the subject of the man who denied her very existence, Sawyer saw his father in her all over again.

She had so many mannerisms that recalled James Marshall. No wonder he hadn't asked for a DNA test.

As they drank, she got more comfortable in her chair, holding her teacup above its saucer. They made small talk, about Sawyer's old job at JMF, about how the New Fortunes Ranch was faring.

But then it was as if the grace period was over, and she got down to brass tacks—another trait that was very James Marshall–esque.

"I imagine that a big sticking point with your brothers and sister was those JMF shares James gave me," she said.

"You'd be right."

She sighed. "I told him that I didn't need his money, but he feels terribly guilty that he has so much and I have so little."

Sawyer merely nodded. She was covering all the bases.

Jeanne Marie put her tea on the table, wearing a wistful smile. "What James doesn't understand is that there are all kinds of riches in the world. I may not have a fat bank account, but I have a loving husband back home, wonderful children and memories I wouldn't sacrifice for a million shares of JMF."

Sawyer smiled, and not just because of her impassioned beliefs. Imagine—he had another uncle. Cousins.

He hadn't really grasped these truths she was telling before now, but there *was* a lot more than just money in this world…and hadn't he experienced one of those things of value last night with Laurel?

Jeanne Marie interrupted the thought, saying, "Honestly, I had no earthly idea that those shares were earmarked for you children. For heaven's sake, all I want to do is tell each and every one of you that you can have them!"

Sawyer agreed. "I think that's a speech my brothers and sister need to hear."

"I wish they'd allow me the chance to give it."

As he watched the woman in front of him, the true-blue sister of James Marshall, his *aunt,* empathy overtook him. The eyes didn't lie, and hers were brimming with a longing to make a case to the family.

And even to be a part of them.

Everything she'd said resonated, and he couldn't stop thinking now about all the riches he had that couldn't be stuffed into a bank account or portfolio: brothers, a sister, cousins—some of whom he didn't even know—and even his parents.

Being a Fortune had benefited him in more ways than just the financial. How long would he have taken his large, colorful family for granted if it hadn't been for this conversation with Jeanne Marie?

As the sun rolled through a window, he thought he noticed a different slant to the light, a different way of recognizing everything around him.

Almost as if he was up in Laurel's plane again.

While Jeanne Marie smiled sadly at him, probably thinking that he didn't have it in him to go to bat for her, he reached across the table and took her hand in his.

"I'm going to see that you get the chance to talk some sense into my brothers and sister," he said. "I promise you that, Aunt Jeanne Marie."

Her eyes welled up at the name, and she squeezed his fingers.

"You can call me Aunt Jeanne, if you'd like. It's shorter. And thank you, Sawyer. We don't get many chances in life, but you can bet that I'm going to take this one by the horns."

Her last words echoed through him, and by the time he left the room, he felt wealthier than ever, with a new aunt, a new uncle, new cousins…

…and a new outlook that was starting to color in the blank spaces Laurel had left him with this morning.

Chapter Nine

Between lessons that day, Laurel took a break, grabbing a turkey sandwich, chips and bottled water from the airport lobby's snack bar and taking a seat in front of the floor-to-ceiling windows.

Here, she could watch the airfield and the planes taxiing, taking off, landing…going places and coming back from them, she thought, sinking down in the chair.

She made an attempt not to think of this morning, trying instead to concentrate on those planes and on the mellow activity of the terminal, where people milled around the posh waiting area and, upstairs, pilots and staff went in and out of the offices. Like the Redmond Flight School building, which was separate from this one, the terminal had suffered a lot of damage during the big tornado, but everything was remodeled now.

Word had it around town that Sawyer, who'd been present for Marcos Mendoza and Wendy Fortune's wedding, had just missed the tornado, already on the road and driving in the opposite direction for some kind of business appointment. Naturally, he'd rushed back to Red Rock to help out in any way he could.

Of course, Laurel hadn't known him back then. But did she really know him now?

More to the point, how well did she know herself?

The old Laurel would've never acted so loony on a morning after, if she'd had many. And she sure wouldn't be sitting here mooning over a guy.

She took a bite of her sandwich. So much for not thinking about Sawyer. But how could she not, when last night had blown her away? Shaken her to the core?

Scared her enough that she'd acted like a complete weirdo this morning.

God, she wouldn't be surprised if she never saw him again, with the way she'd just about sprinted right out the door this morning. *I'm going to take off, if you don't mind. Just lock the door from inside on the knob when you leave?*

She cringed even now. How socially awkward. He probably thought she was like a rookie who'd been passed the football during a big game and had run the wrong way on the field.

The sandwich stuck in her throat. She washed it down with the water, then put the food aside.

What a mess she was, caught between fearing that she had let Sawyer get too close to her last night and fearing that she had pushed him too far away this morning.

Had she meant to do that, though? Push him away?

Had she been testing him to see if he would come back, even when she was at her worst?

She stared at the aircraft, wishing she could just fly all day, far away from her issues, coming back to a time before she'd decided to say yes to Sawyer.

Because that would make her life easier, wouldn't it?

Or would it make it…

Less interesting, she thought. *A hell of a lot less interesting.*

A male voice sounded behind her. "It looks like you're a million miles away."

She turned to see her brother, his dark eyes framed by smile lines. He was holding a sandwich and a soda, obviously grabbing a bite to eat, too.

Gesturing to a seat next to her, Laurel said, "Are you here to crack the whip on me, Tanner?"

"I'm not that much of a hard-case boss." He sat. "Am I?"

She laughed, shaking her head.

As he unwrapped a BLT, he nodded toward the airfield. "This is where I always find you when you're doing some soul searching."

She blinked at him. "What're you talking about?"

"You haven't worked here long, but I've noticed a pattern. You're here every time something reminds you of Steve, like an especially trying phone call from Juliet. You were even here after you finished unpacking a box that accidentally had one of our father's old shirts in it."

The clothing hadn't been anything sentimental to her; she must've grabbed it out of a rag pile at their mother's place without thinking while she was packing up some Disney figurines she'd bought at a garage sale when she was five and then stored at Mom's.

But it'd been a shock to look at that piece of flannel

when she'd been unpacking for her new apartment here, then realizing who it'd belonged to. She'd walked it to the Dumpster right away, thinking that her trash can was even too good for it.

"So why're you daydreaming in front of this window today?" Tanner asked.

"You don't want to hear it."

He put his sandwich back in its wrapper. "If Sawyer—"

"He didn't do anything wrong." He'd done everything *right*. Too right.

"Then I don't get it, Laurel. What's with the long face?"

She glanced at Tanner. He was worried about her, and she didn't want him to be.

After blowing out a breath, she said, "It's just that I've gotten closer to Sawyer than I planned."

"I see. Plans. You're real big on those."

She had been, until Sawyer had made most of them fly out the window. "It's not that I don't care for him. I do. And that's the problem."

"I get it. The thought of trusting someone again is daunting."

"Big-time."

"Then stop seeing him."

There must've been a flicker of helpless emotion that crossed her face, because Tanner cursed under his breath.

"You didn't," he said.

"I'm not going to tell you what I did or didn't do." Sex. Hot sex. Sex that'd sent her into a dither on the morning after, when she'd had time to absorb all the emotions that were overcoming her.

"Didn't you two have some kind of shared philosophy when this all started?" Tanner asked. "Some anti-marriage crusade?"

She nodded. But something stirred in her, and as a plane sped down the runway outside, winging into the air, she realized what that stirring was.

What if she truly wasn't antimarriage?

Good God, didn't everyone—even her—long to be loved, even if they hid it? To be cherished in a way they'd never been cherished before?

She didn't dare tell Tanner, because then it would all come tumbling out of her—the doubts that she'd covered up about maybe not being worthy of that kind of affection.

For all her outward accomplishments, she really didn't have any faith that someone would stick by her for the long haul, did she?

She didn't even have faith in Sawyer. And that's why she would never believe that he could be someone long-term, even if he'd looked at her with his heart and soul in his eyes last night. Even if every touch, every kiss transcended "fun" or "benefits."

In spite of all the negative thoughts consuming her, one little ray of hope bled through: *Was* it too much to wish for someone who would unconditionally stick by her someday?

Even now, just asking it, she shrank into her shell, pushing away from the little bit of hope she'd had before anyone else could tear her apart.

Tanner had clearly been weighing his next words

carefully. "I wish I had some solid big-brother advice up my sleeve, but I don't. All I can tell you is that there're a lot of people who start off thinking that love isn't in the cards because they've been dinged by relationships before. Jordana and I didn't even start off on a perfect note."

That was true. Jordana had gotten stranded with Tanner during the tornado, and they'd given in to the urge for danger sex, fueled by adrenaline and the fear of not surviving to see the morning.

Then he'd heard that Jordana was pregnant. Then... the rest was history. Her brother had gone to Atlanta, pursuing the woman who was carrying his child, even though he'd been angry that she'd hidden the news from him, and their love had blossomed from there.

No, Tanner hadn't been built for love at first, because he'd had the same useless father Laurel had. He'd had the same hang-ups.

But here he was, smiling, as if he'd started thinking of his wife and their son, Jack.

"You know," she said, her throat tight, "that was some pretty damned good advice right now, whether you meant for it to be or not."

As he rested a hand on her shoulder, she thought, *Now, if I just knew what the hell to do with that advice...*

When Sawyer walked into his dining room, he found Shane and Lia already there, eating a lunch of black-bean quesadillas, salad and fries.

They were grouped at the far end of the table, and a place setting was waiting for Sawyer, who was wearing a smile as he sat.

"Something's up," Shane said to Lia, who was resting her hand on her round tummy.

"It's the smile," Lia said. "Always the smile."

Since she and Sawyer had mended their fences after the whole gold-digger situation, he felt free to give her a cheerful wink. "It's been a good day."

"And apparently a good night," Shane said, taking a bite of his quesadilla.

Naturally, they'd noticed that he hadn't been around until morning, when he'd come here to shower, hop into a change of clothes, then take off to see Jeanne Marie.

Shane didn't know about that last part, though. Not yet.

Lia was waggling her dark eyebrows. "Did you and Laurel Redmond…?"

Sawyer shrugged. A gentleman never told.

But a gentleman certainly couldn't get a lady off his mind, either. All day he'd worn a grin on his face, like an addled fool.

Lightheartedness wasn't the only thing swaying him, though. A more serious side kept recalling Aunt Jeanne's words. *We don't get many chances in life, but you can bet that I'm going to take this one by the horns.*

He'd decided that this should be the way he approached Laurel, too. After last night, he felt like a new man, and hearing Aunt Jeanne's outlook on life had only encouraged him.

It was true that he'd come to Red Rock to reinvent himself, just as his brothers had done, yet he'd realized today that reinvention might not be so necessary when he'd been this man all along. Someone who loved his family.

Someone who'd just learned how much he appreciated everything he had.

He'd actually been committed to family before, so why had *commitment* been such a dirty word with women? Maybe independence didn't have to extend as far as he'd been taking it with Laurel, either.

Now if he could only get her to see the same light.

As Shane finished up his food, Sawyer said, "I have more than one reason to smile."

"And that would be...?" Shane asked.

He readied himself for Shane's reaction to the news of the Jeanne Marie visit.

"I dropped by Aunt Jeanne's today," he said, tearing off the proverbial bandage with one swift rip.

Shane put down the napkin he'd been using to wipe his mouth. The way he did it was so careful that Lia sat up straighter in her chair.

Sawyer braced himself even more.

"Aunt Jeanne," Shane said. "Is that what she wants you to call her?"

"She liked the sound of it. So do I."

"Dammit, Sawyer."

"What? What the hell is wrong with you that you're icing out a woman who's no doubt related to Dad?"

Shane's face went ruddy, and Sawyer decided that a gentler approach might be in order.

Lia must've been thinking the same thing. "Shane..."

He looked at her, his gaze filled with an emotion that made Sawyer think that his brother had talked to Lia about Aunt Jeanne at length.

Affection took the place of everything else in Shane's

eyes as he sent a tender smile to his fiancée. Then he nodded.

"I know," he said to Sawyer, "that yesterday, during the meeting, you brought up how we treated Lia when she first showed up here pregnant. You both know I regret how I responded."

"Me, too." Sawyer slid a glance to Lia. She was half grinning, as if proud of Shane for cooling off and sorting through his emotions about Jeanne.

Shane sat back in his chair. "You were right in comparing how I treated Lia to how I should be handling Jeanne Marie."

Sawyer imagined how happy Jeanne would be if she was here to listen in.

"All she wants," he said, "is to make her case to every one of us—and it's not because she's some kind of masterful con artist who has a silver tongue. We've got cousins, Shane, and another uncle—Jeanne Marie's husband. We've got a whole other family that we never knew about."

"Okay." Shane connected gazes with Lia, who looked very pleased. "I'll meet with her."

"You might even end up calling her Aunt Jeanne by the time you're done," Sawyer said.

As Shane chuckled wryly, Lia got up from the table, her smile at full force now as she held her plate and headed for the kitchen. "I'll leave you to tease each other."

"You just want to see what's for dessert," Shane said as they touched hands while she passed by, then disappeared into the kitchen with a yeah-you're-right laugh.

"Who knew?" Shane said. "Her appetite has grown

tenfold this past week alone. I'm marrying an Olympic-caliber eater, Sawyer."

"Just one more thing to adore about her, right?"

Shane got a curious gleam in his eye, and Sawyer knew where this discussion was leading.

"Now that we got business out of the way…" Shane said. "We were talking about you and Laurel…?"

Sawyer couldn't fight the grin.

"Ha!" Shane pointed at him. "See—you've been zapped right in the butt by the Red Rock Plague, as you call it."

"I'm not…" He'd been about to say "in love with Laurel."

But what *did* love feel like? And how was he supposed to know when it really was love?

"This is so Shakespeare," Shane said. "Did you ever read *The Taming of the Shrew* in school?"

"That play about the guy who has to court the nasty-tongued woman so he can get her dowry? Tell me you're not comparing Laurel to a shrew."

"You have to admit that she has a bit of a reputation. But you're right—as I sit here looking at you, I wonder if you tamed her or if she tamed you."

"That's hilarious, Shane."

But he turned over the comparison in his head as his brother cleared his plate and got up to join Lia in the kitchen.

He was right. Just who was being tamed here?

Sawyer watched Shane go, and a faint, familiar feeling of being left behind dogged him. He would rather have died than ever admit it to his siblings, but throughout his life, he'd always been the one who trailed the others. The pattern had even repeated itself here in Red Rock, where Shane, Asher and Wyatt had discovered who they were and found the women of their dreams in quick succession.

Was it possible that what Sawyer was feeling for Laurel wasn't…well, real? Was he still playing catch-up with his brothers in a way?

Was that the reason these emotions for Laurel had come upon him so rapidly, so strongly? Because he wanted them to?

With that on his mind, he ate the rest of his lunch alone, missing Laurel.

Wanting to see her just as soon as he could, no matter what the reason might be.

When Laurel's phone rang that evening and she glimpsed Sawyer's name on the ID screen, her body felt such a mighty shock that she thought she'd accidentally tripped over a live wire.

More, she thought, the word encompassing everything her body was feeling. More ramped-up hormones, more high-flying sex.

But along with the joy of knowing he was on the other end of the line, scary words attacked her, too. Words like *commitment, betrayal, trust.*

Where did one end and where did another begin?

Her body won out, and she found herself answering, keeping her tone level as she sat on her sofa.

"Hello?"

"Hey, Laur." He sounded confident, as if he hadn't noticed that she'd gone nutso on him this morning. "I thought I'd call to see what you're doing."

It wasn't hard to figure out what he was actually saying: *I know you can't stop thinking of me.*

But he'd been thinking of her, too, right?

"I'm off work now," she said. "It was another long day."

"You hungry?"

Always—whether it was for birthday cake or him. But she merely said, "I had a late lunch."

"That's fine, because they're trying out a new tapas menu at Red."

Tapas. She was a sucker for the small Spanish plates, mostly because they allowed you to sample a bunch of food during one meal, and you didn't have to order a gargantuan serving if you weren't that hungry.

But she'd hesitated in answering, and Sawyer picked up on it. "You have to eat sometime."

It wasn't eating she was worried about. Yet she wanted to go. She couldn't deny it.

Then the voice of reason smoothed over her, assuring her that her hormones were only on overdrive. Last night had been their first night together, and there was bound to be a burst of happy adrenaline that she'd misconstrued to be something...else.

Wasn't this a chance to prove those hormones wrong by going with him tonight?

"What time?" she asked.

She could tell he was smiling. "I can pick you up in twenty."

Make him work. "How about forty?"

He laughed. "Forty it is. See you soon."

She hung up, her pulse nattering away, like little gossips gathered in her veins, talking at her.

You've done it now. Good luck avoiding his bedroom eyes. Ready to be crushed again?

But even above those sounds, she *felt* rather than heard. And the urges were giddy and addictive.

She wouldn't have to give in to anything more than those temporary urges.

It's just dinner, she thought. That was all it'd be.

She dressed as if she could care less what Sawyer would think—a yellow cotton shirt stitched with a border of beads around the dipped collar, nice jeans, boots. She swept her hair up in a barrette, leaving careless spiky strands above the twist. A swipe of lip balm and she was ready.

Then she sat in front of the TV. Nothing seemed to be on, even though she had a hundred or so channels to choose from.

Why had she told him forty minutes again?

Oh, yeah—to make him wait.

Since when did Laurel Redmond play games like this?

She knew since when, and she didn't like the answer. Long ago she'd promised herself that she would never change for any man. She would live on her terms.

And she wasn't liking these terms.

When Sawyer rang her doorbell, she jumped off the sofa, then chilled herself out, forcing herself to walk slowly to the door. She opened it and tried not to blush when he gave her a lazy, appreciative look, just like last night.

But this wouldn't be another last night.

She smiled. They were going to have fun. Nothing else involved.

"Ready?" she asked, starting out the door before he could answer.

"Ready," he said.

His legs were so long that he didn't have any problem getting to his Jag before she did, and he opened her door for her. She slid inside, efficiently doing up her seat belt.

Act normal. Act fun. "Did you know that tapas came about because of a king?"

Small talk. It definitely put her back on track with Sawyer.

He started the engine, then backed out of the parking spot. "Is this another of your random travel facts? Like the one you told me about Cologne, Germany?"

"I'm full of them." And she was far more comfortable now.

"Then give it to me. What's a king have to do with tapas?"

"They say that Alfonso the Tenth of Castile was getting over a sickness by drinking wine and eating small dishes between every meal."

"Sounds like a king."

"Always indulging, right? And after he got better, he commanded that the taverns couldn't serve wine unless there were snacks that came with it. A 'tapa.'"

"Did you get ahold of that trivia before or after you were in Spain?"

They were cruising the road now, the top down, the breeze soothing her.

"I was actually in Spain when I heard it. You've been there?"

"Just once."

"It has a different kind of social life, doesn't it?

Things don't get lively until around midnight, but you're ready for it because you sleep in the afternoon during siesta, when just about everything shuts down."

"Which cities did you visit?"

"Seville, Barcelona, Madrid. The basics. But someday…"

"You'd like to go back. Me, too."

Before he could do something romantic like invite her to take off with him in a jet, she changed the subject.

Surprise! But as she babbled about the kinds of flowers and trees they were seeing on the side of the road, he went with it once again.

Easygoing Sawyer, she thought, her heart thudding. She liked that about him.

Liked it…a lot.

By the time they arrived at the restaurant, it was dinnertime and Red was crowded to the brim. Evidently Sawyer had called ahead, because they were whisked through the main room, with its Southwestern-style antiques and blankets covering the walls. A converted hacienda that had historically been owned by a high-class Spanish family, Red was the restaurant of choice in town, as the hustle and bustle attested to.

The hostess seated them in the courtyard, near the splashing tiled fountain and under the Mexican fan trees, and she left them with the tapas menu.

The waiter came to them soon afterward, greeting Sawyer first.

"Mr. Fortune, so good to see you again."

"Thanks, Abel. Do you know Laurel?"

Abel, who was dark-haired and brown-eyed and had a bright smile, turned to Laurel.

"I haven't had the pleasure. May I get you a wine list?"

Laurel demurred, and Sawyer ordered a beer. But before Abel left, he gave Laurel and Sawyer a...well, all Laurel could call it was a look.

Like they were together.

Nerves flung themselves against Laurel's skin. They *were* together, but that didn't mean a serious kind of together. Why couldn't she just get that through her head and enjoy it?

Because you're setting yourself up, she thought. *And you're walking into this trap as if you want the pain that you know will come.*

But she didn't want to listen to all that negativity anymore, not when Sawyer's eyes were sparkling as he combed over the tapas menu in anticipation of sharing something with her.

Not when she wanted so badly to be here with him, no matter the consequences.

Chapter Ten

By the time Sawyer brought Laurel back to his convertible in Red's parking lot, night had veiled the sky.

She sat in the seat, holding her stomach. "I just knew I was going to eat too much."

"They didn't exactly have a shortage of great dishes on the menu. I have a feeling it'll take another trip or two to try everything we wanted."

"Ugh. Maybe we shouldn't talk about eating."

She smiled at him, her head back against the seat. All night he'd been hungering to reach over, undo her barrette and let her hair fall down her back.

But she still seemed a little distant, as if she was here with him, having a great time, but...

She was cautious.

Since he knew about her past with that Steve idiot and her father, Sawyer wasn't all that stunned. Plus, he could work with cautious. He didn't have to rush right into bed with her again. Maybe a night of pure and simple romance, of being with her just for the hell of it, would put them back to normal again.

Leaning an arm on the steering wheel, he returned her smile. "Once, a wise woman told me that she knew what I needed. And I think I know what she could use right about now."

There went that wary gaze of hers again.

"Don't worry, Laur," he said. "I'll be a good boy."

After he started the engine and drove, he could feel her watching him out of the corner of her eye, probably wondering what he had in mind.

He headed in the direction of New Fortunes Ranch, then passed the entrance by about a mile or so. When he slowed down, it finally became possible for him to hear her over the wind.

"I'm assuming you know where you're going?" she asked loudly.

"Somewhere down property." He pulled into a turnoff at the side of the road. It was shaded by pines, marked by the sound of owls.

He shut the engine down, and they both got out. After he went to his trunk to get a flashlight, he led her toward the entrance to a trail.

"What's this?" she asked.

"I found it one day when I was scouting out the area. It's a rough hiking trail, and I think it's just what you need to walk off some of those tapas."

"Just look at you, Sawyer Fortune. You can be a wise person yourself."

If she was surprised that he hadn't urged her straight

into bed, she didn't show it. But that cautious vibe still lingered.

Was she actually relieved to stay away from intimacy tonight?

Patience, Sawyer told himself. She was worth his time.

He turned on the flashlight, the beam dancing over the rough evergreen trunks and rocks. Some hiker had been kind enough to mark the trail by piling stones as landmarks.

"We won't go too far in," Sawyer said.

She laughed. "Are you afraid we'll get lost?"

"I'm a careful man."

"You do know you're with someone who's gone through all sorts of survival scenarios. I never saw as much trouble as Tanner did overseas, but I had occasion to use my skills. I learned everything I ever needed during all my military training."

He ran the light over her as they walked. Athletic, graceful, a lady who could kick butt at a moment's notice. Was there anything she couldn't do?

"Is boot camp as hard as they say?" he asked.

"It's where the studs are separated from the duds, if you know what I mean. I went to officer's training instead of regular boot camp, but either way, you get used to what's required of you each day. And if you don't?" She made a neck-cutting motion, along with the sound effect, then grinned at him.

"What do you do during all that training?"

"At first, you wake up, do PT—physical training— eat, train, eat, learn things like military history and more

in a classroom, eat, prepare for the next day, then sleep…
and that's just in general."

This woman put him and his gym workouts to shame.
As smart as she was—and as good as she was at seemingly everything—why was she hanging out with *him*?

He couldn't help feeling kind of proud that he'd
passed her standards.

But how long would that last?

A tiny piece of hope inside of him piped up. *Could
it last?*

They weren't too far down the trail when he found
what he'd ultimately wanted to show her out here.

He combed the light over what looked to be the limestone foundation of a small house that had been de-
stroyed.

Laurel was immediately enthralled, and she hotfooted
it over to the empty square of stone.

"Please tell me you know the story that goes along
with this," she said.

"I might know a little something." When he'd first
found the ruins, he'd done a bit of online research. "There
was a couple who supposedly settled here around the
1850s. You probably know that there used to be stage-
coach routes that ran out of San Antonio."

"Yup." She'd gone past the barrier of limestone and
was inside the abandoned square now.

"I guess there was a bachelor who got off at the near-
est stop and decided he liked the looks of things, so he
stayed. He fell for the daughter of the innkeeper where
he was staying and built her this place. But they say
that one day the two of them just up and disappeared,

their house gutted. No one knows what really happened to them."

Laurel had bent down to investigate the remnants of a fireplace mantel, and sent him a slow look over her shoulder. "Are you trying to scare me with a ghost story?"

Sawyer had a good laugh at that. "I think it'd take a full-scale *War of the Worlds* alien invasion to scare you." He rethought that. "I take that back. You'd be the rebel leader who storms the mother ship."

They laughed together, and he joined her inside the square of rock. Then she stood and put her hands on her hips, as if she was imagining the room with chairs, people, life. He saw how she approached every new experience, with wonderment and total immersion.

"I swear, Sawyer, I have no idea what to make of you sometimes."

Join the club. "What do you mean?"

"You brought me out here for an entirely different reason than I thought."

"And what did you think?"

"That you found some amazing make-out spot and you were going to…"

"Seduce you?" He hooked his free thumb in a belt loop. "Come on, Laurel. Don't you know that I think there's more to you than what we did last night? You're different from any other woman I've met, and if you haven't guessed it by now, I kind of like that about you."

The atmosphere had gone serious, and he was pretty sure she was assessing him. But since the trees were hiding the moon and he couldn't very well shine the flashlight on her face to see her expression, he wasn't sure what she was thinking.

He decided to throw a bit of levity into the situation. "Besides, I thought it'd just plain be a good time to show you this place. I'm afraid there's not going to be a hell of a lot of opportunity for traipsing around the woods during the next couple of weeks, what with my brothers' wedding preparations and all."

"Ah, yes, the wedding."

"I'm sure you're just as tired of hearing about it as I am thinking of it."

She started to say something, then stopped. But then she went ahead.

"I'm just going to put this out there, Sawyer, and you tell me if I'm wrong. Am I part of some big life experiment for you? I know you wanted a different existence out here in Red Rock, and sometimes it seems that I'm a part of that change."

It was true that he'd come out west to find himself, but she had it all wrong. "Do you think I'm just testing a different kind of woman than I'm used to and seeing how you fit into this new life I've got? Because that's not the case."

"Then how about this—you're the only brother who's not getting married, so every time you mention them, it sounds like you feel a little out of it. Like you really are that younger brother who doesn't belong." She paused. "And you want to belong, so you're bringing me to abandoned homesteads in the woods and taking me out to dinner and…" She let her comment fade.

Was she *looking* for excuses to make their relationship rocky?

Still, she'd nailed him, gotten his number, however you wanted to put it. Because he'd been wondering the same about himself.

Yet just hearing her say all that, he knew her theories couldn't be true. He sincerely did like Laurel for being Laurel.

Why did he get the feeling that it was hard for her to accept that?

"Wow," he said. "You realize that you just suggested that my brothers all have significant others now and I'm only with you because I don't want to be left out."

She just stared at him. He could sense it, even in the near dark.

Then she started laughing. He did, too, more out of relief than anything.

"Do you want to just leave me in the woods?" she asked jokingly. "That way you won't have to hear me run my mouth anymore."

He wanted to tell her that he could be the one man who understood all her issues—that he knew she was only being guarded because of what she'd been through with her dad and her ex. That he would give her time to sort through what she needed to.

But as if she wanted to avoid any more talk, she jumped over the limestone barrier, going back to the trail.

"Do you plan to become a permanent part of the structure or what?" she asked. "Come on, Fortune."

At the sound of his last name, his stomach sank.

Time, he thought. If there was one thing he'd learned lately, it was that anything worth pursuing would take time.

And more and more, he knew that Laurel would be worth the trouble.

* * *

Even a few days later, Laurel still had Sawyer and their trip to the woods on her mind.

Or more to the point, she kept going over what'd happened *afterward*.

Sawyer had driven her home, and if things had been slightly awkward between them when she'd accused him of using her because he wanted to be like his brothers, that had been just a warm-up.

After he'd parked his car, she'd been caught between inviting him inside and saying a simple good-night. Her libido was begging for one while her brain was demanding the other.

Luckily, Sawyer had gotten a call from Shane, and his family drama had taken the pressure off her.

"Evidently," he'd said, putting away his phone as they'd sat in the car, "my brother made good on his promise to contact Aunt Jeanne at La Casa Paloma Hotel, and he's asking if I'd like to join them in the bar for a nightcap."

Was someone watching out for her or what? Laurel had been torn between libido and brain all night, yearning for Sawyer, then telling herself that she would only be digging herself into a deeper hole with him if they ended up in bed again.

"Don't feel bad about going to them," she said. "I know how important this is."

"You could come with me."

But Laurel knew a good opportunity when it presented itself. "No worries, Fortune. I've got an early morning, anyway."

At her use of his last name, he frowned a bit, just as

he had earlier. And every time she said it, she cursed herself, even though it was the most effective intimacy blocker she could think of.

They'd kissed good-night—of course, she'd been drawn to him like a magnet and had found it almost impossible to drag herself away—but that was it.

Her body sure hadn't been happy with her afterward. A sharp craving had haunted her all night.

A well-deserved one.

And her run of luck only continued. For the next few days, Sawyer had been swept up in his brothers' wedding preparations, getting last-minute alterations to his best man's tux, seeing to the details of the reception, which would be held at the gazebo on New Fortunes Ranch.

But she hadn't realized how much she would miss him until it was actually happening. It was a sore, awful, terrible emptiness that only he could fill.

That frightened her, too, because when no-strings Sawyer inevitably lost interest in their little affair, no matter what she thought she saw in his eyes when he looked at her, it would devastate her. She would end up resembling that decimated limestone house they'd come across in the woods the other night.

Ruined. Unsuitable for living. A repeat of how she'd felt after Steve had screwed her over.

Today, though, she wasn't feeling so hollow. She was off work and waiting for a knock on the door.

When she heard it, she rushed to answer, and as soon as she threw the door open, she was gushing with the kind of happiness a proud aunt carried around.

"Jack!" she said, going straight for the chubby-cheeked baby in her brother's arms.

The little boy had a smile that stretched across his face as he leaned away from his dad and reached toward her.

"Okay, then," Tanner said, laughing as Laurel pulled Jack against her, holding him and cupping the back of his head, kissing his baby softness. "Now I know what it's like to cease existing."

"Hi, to you, too, Tanner," Laurel said between kisses. She drew back and looked at her nephew's darling face, unable to stop a goofy smile that seemed to take her over every time she saw him.

Tanner dropped his son's diaper bag near the inside of the door. "You should have everything in here. Jordana says thanks a million. Me, too."

"Tell her hi for me, and thank you for letting me take care of Jack. Besides, parents need to have time alone, especially busy parents."

"In other words, you're always available."

"You got it," Laurel said, resting her cheek against Jack's head.

Tanner didn't go just yet. It was hard for him and Jordana to be away from Jack, but Laurel had already become a pro at this babysitting thing. Still, the couple never spent more than a few hours away from their son, and today was no exception. They were only going for a meal in town.

Tanner finally kissed Jack goodbye, and Laurel distracted her nephew with smitten-auntie faces so he wouldn't fuss about Daddy leaving him behind.

But the child didn't have the Redmond complex about crappy fathers—and Laurel was sure he never would, seeing as Tanner was already Dad of the Year in her book.

When Tanner was gone, Laurel walked around her apartment with Jack. "What do you think, buddy? You want to play choo-choo?" He liked sitting on the carpet and having Laurel grab his ankles, pulling him along as she went, "Choo-choo!"

Instead of answering, he was fiddling with a button on her shirt. So much for choo-choo.

She decided to take him outside, to the small playground attached to the apartment complex. They had their choice of a swing set, a sandbox and a bouncing horsey.

While holding him on top of the metal animal, she was in the middle of creating the appropriate whinnying sound effects when her phone dinged.

She wrapped an arm around Jack to steady him, accessing the text.

Sawyer.

Something in her chest spun like a whirring top as she read the message.

Haven't seen you for a while. Dinner?

Yesyesyesyes, her libido said. But her brain disagreed.

She ignored her head, too excited to listen to it. She and Sawyer could have a late dinner after Tanner and Jordana picked up Jack, right? They could sit around and watch TV, kiss, neck, be happy with each other's company. It didn't have to go any further tonight.

Or if it did, she would handle it, enjoying their time together for what it was.

Couldn't she do that?

As she texted back a time—8:00 p.m.?—her whole body felt as if it was twirling now.

I've got a better idea, said Sawyer's next text. You at home?

Yes.

Good. Missed you.

And that was all he wrote. When she texted back a question mark, he didn't answer.

Why did she have the feeling that push-the-envelope Sawyer wasn't going to wait until eight?

She admitted that she didn't want him to, anyway, and scooped Jack off the play horse, taking him to the sandbox.

He was a creative child, if Laurel said so herself, and time passed quickly as he pushed the sand into piles that he pounded into shapes she didn't quite understand yet. Although in his smart little mind, they probably made all the sense in the world.

She bent over to kiss Jack's temple. There weren't enough kisses in the world for him, really, and sometimes she thought that she could spend all night just cuddling and kissing his soft cheek.

"Who loves you, buddy?" she asked. "Me. That's who."

Jack laughed. She stroked his cheek, and when she sat down again, she realized that they hadn't been alone.

When she saw Sawyer, her heart jerked.

Then her entire body caught fire.

He had a look on his face that told her he'd been moved by what he'd seen with her and Jack, and that he was possibly thinking things that he shouldn't be thinking about her and children.

But she had to be wrong about that, because this

was Sawyer Fortune, the playboy, the survivor of the Plague....

He snapped out of it, holding up a takeout bag from Red.

"Let me guess," she said, trying to steady her voice. God, she'd missed him. "You brought the tapas we didn't get to try the other night."

"Right on target." He came to the sandbox, his gaze on Jack, his second cousin.

"Hey, there," he said, getting to a knee.

When Jack's face lit up the same as it did every time he saw Laurel, she sat back and watched.

Sawyer was a natural, as if he'd been around children all his life and knew just how to relate. Not long ago, she would've said that Sawyer got along with kids because he was really one himself, but that didn't ring true right now.

Not as her heart pounded from the center of a warm ring—a circle that didn't seem to be protecting her as much as it was enveloping her.

She forced the feeling away and bent to Jack. "What do you say? Are you hungry?"

He made an eating motion with his hand. Baby sign language.

Sawyer chuckled. "I'd say so. Do you think his eating habits will be as cultured and adventurous as his aunt's?"

"He's more into bland pureed stuff right now, but we're getting there."

Sawyer rounded up Jack before Laurel could do so, and the boy seemed so tiny in the crook of his arm that her heart softened. Jack also looked ecstatic to be with Sawyer, grabbing at his embroidered shirt collar.

"He'll be a nice dresser," Sawyer said. "I can tell that he's into clothes already. I'll have to introduce him to my tailor."

They walked back to her apartment and Laurel took the prepared food from Jack's diaper bag and laid it out on the table. Meanwhile, Sawyer worked on the adult grub, undoing the takeout containers and forking the tapas onto plates.

As they ate together, with Laurel feeding Jack, a forbidden fantasy came to her.

A family. Three of them, a mom, a dad, a baby...

At one point Sawyer met her gaze, and she looked away when she thought she saw the fantasy reflected in him.

But this was ridiculous. It was easy to babysit. It was quite another thing to wake up in the middle of the night because your baby was crying and to worry that your marriage was breaking apart from the stress.

Because that's what marriage would be. Stress after the honeymoon was over. Besides, she'd always told herself that she'd have a child on her own terms one day, after she got back on her financial feet. And she'd let Sawyer know on the first night they'd met that she wanted to adopt or go to a sperm bank.

There was no fantasy here.

When Tanner and Jordana arrived to pick up Jack, she was sorry to see him go. Then again, having a child around with Sawyer present did make things ten times more awkward.

And when Tanner greeted Sawyer, it was awkward times a thousand.

Jordana took Jack in her arms, her cheeks flushed at

seeing her child. It was obvious she had struggled with being away from him, even for a couple of hours. Tanner couldn't even stop touching his son's head, smoothing back his wispy hair.

"Thank you so much," Jordana said to both Laurel and Sawyer, as if they were a team. "We had a great time."

"You just call when you want another date," Laurel said.

When he and Jordana left, Tanner sent one last curious glance over his shoulder at Sawyer, but Laurel shut the door before Sawyer could see.

Hopefully.

And…yes. He'd already gone to clear the table, sauntering into the kitchen and throwing garbage away.

Now that they were alone, she wanted to rush over to him, lay the kiss of all kisses on him. All her plans about merely cuddling on the couch and smooching with him completely poofed into thin air.

When she'd had those milder thoughts, she had forgotten how much she wanted him. Being alone with him, here, now, definitely reminded her.

She joined him in the kitchen, as he was turned to the sink and was rinsing dishes. Just as he'd done on their morning after, she wrapped her arms around his waist.

"It's been too long," she said, hugging him to her chest.

Fun. Flirty. No attachments.

She'd make sure that's all tonight would be about.

The moment Sawyer felt Laurel pressing against his back, he lost it.

Control. That's what he needed, and he searched for some.

But if she could read his mind to see what he was thinking and feeling right now, she'd run.

These past few days, he'd ached for her. It didn't matter what hour it was, his chest literally hurt when he thought of her.

But he hadn't had time with the wedding preparations to see her, and even though he would call her or text her, this game they were playing was beginning to wear on him. It was starting to etch deep grooves into his core, like tires that were spinning and burning and getting nowhere.

As she laid a palm flat on his belly, he nearly cursed. The effect was that brutal, like a pulsating jab of needles in his gut and groin.

And in his heart, he thought, unable to deny it any longer.

She slipped her hand down a bit more, over his fly, and he sucked in a breath.

"Did you miss me, too?" she whispered.

"You know I did."

"Good." She caressed him, already making him hard.

How could she be so cavalier about this?

Then again, how could she not, when he'd tried to cover how he was really feeling, just so he wouldn't scare her off?

He was going to burst if she kept on handling him like this, so he turned around, cupping her face in his hands, stopping her.

He didn't even say anything, just looked deep into her eyes.

But Laurel was Laurel, and she only smiled as if this was still casual, still a game.

"It's been a while since you've seen my room," she said, taking his hand and pulling him away from the sink. "Why don't we see if it's changed at all?"

"Laurel…"

Frustrated, he couldn't stand it anymore, pulling her into his arms, kissing her slowly, showing her what he couldn't put into words.

At first she didn't move, only raised her hands in the air as if she were helpless, caught in a net. Then, for a beautiful moment, she responded, swaying into him, her hands gripping his arms.

He'd always known how to make her weak, but he didn't want to break her down—he wanted to build her up, to show her that she didn't have to worry about being betrayed by him.

That he was the man for her.

But just as she began to lose herself in the kiss, she ended it, took hold of his shirt and hauled him toward the bedroom.

"Just come on, cowboy," she said, getting him all the way into her room.

At least she hadn't called him Fortune, but he feared that was next.

"Laurel," he said, his voice grainy, "maybe we should take a breath here."

"There's plenty of time for breathing later." She was already stripping off her shirt, undoing her pants, pulling off her boots. "You're lagging, Fortune."

Dammit, there it was.

She must've seen the frustration in him, because she avoided his gaze, grabbing ahold of his shirt again and, with flirty concentration, unbuttoning it.

"If it's been a long day for you," she said, yanking the material off him and going for his jeans next, "I'll make it better."

"I don't need better...I just need—"

She stood on her tiptoes and pressed her mouth against his, cutting him off, kissing him so hard and so thoroughly that he was the helpless one, holding her arms as he fell further and further into his emotions.

This was it. *She* was it, and he would never find anyone who matched him so perfectly.

Why couldn't she see that?

Why couldn't she stop fighting what was so damned obvious?

He wasn't wearing anything now, so he was utterly revealed as she pulled him toward the bed and turned him around at the same time. Just after he fell backward onto the mattress, she climbed on top of him, clad only in her plain white bra and panties.

"You're awful quiet, Fortune," she said, and she almost sounded desperate as she sat atop his stiffness, closing her eyes.

He almost let go of every ounce of control right then, with her against him, with the blood pounding so hard between his legs that his brain nearly turned to smoke.

But that name she'd called him—Fortune, not Sawyer, not who he really was—was the last straw.

"Don't call me that, Laurel," he said. "Do you know what it sounds like?"

She pushed her hair back, widening her eyes, as if she didn't know. But he saw fright in her gaze.

And he couldn't live with that or the fear of commitment any longer.

He framed her face with his hands again, holding her like the most precious element on earth.

"Don't you see that I love you?"

Chapter Eleven

The word batted at her again and again—in the head, in the heart.

Love.

As in "I love you."

She almost forced a clueless smile to her lips, mostly out of a need to brush off his comment, but more out of an urge to pretend that he was just joking around and that any second he would start kidding about them being the sole survivors of the Plague again.

But judging by his face—the blue eyes filled with affection, the rawness of his entire expression—he wasn't playing.

As she gaped at him, he started talking.

"You didn't expect to hear that." His laugh was short and quiet as he stroked his thumbs over her cheeks. "I didn't expect to say it."

An anesthetic feeling swallowed her as she wrapped

her fingers around his wrists, slowly bringing his hands away from her face. "You weren't supposed to say it."

It sounded so dumb, as if she was accusing him of cheating at the rules of a game when this wasn't a game. Had it ever been?

He didn't react for a second as her last words floated in the air, an invisible wedge between them.

An odd thought came to Laurel: one of them could save the moment right now by making a real jest of all this, by shrugging and pretending that this had never happened and continuing on with where they'd been going on this bed.

By changing the subject, which she did so well.

Backing away from him, she got off the mattress and lightly said, "You almost got me there, Fortune."

Using his last name was a last-ditch effort, and it had its intended effect.

"You actually can't say my name," he said. "Does it make you feel too close to me or something?"

"Don't make an issue out of it." She picked up his jeans from the floor, tossed them over his lap and went about fetching hers and methodically putting them on. "I think it's time to call it a night."

Cool, calm. Surviving.

Always surviving. Because just look what was happening—the fallout. The ugliness she'd always known would come, even with a good time.

"Look at me, Laurel." Sawyer hadn't moved from the bed.

She did look at him, and even as she made sure her expression was unaffected, panic was eating her alive.

Don't you see that I love you?

Why had he said it, dammit?

It seemed as if pure emotion was gnawing at him, too, his blue eyes piercing her.

"I'm not sorry I admitted it." His voice was strong, as if he thought he could turn her heart around. "I've been feeling this way for a while."

"But my reaction isn't what you hoped it'd be?" She buttoned up her jeans, bent down, snagged her shirt off the floor. "What did you expect?"

"I don't know. For you to realize that you felt something for me, too?"

She pulled her shirt over her head. "I thought we were clear from the beginning—no strings."

"And I thought that would be easy enough…until it wasn't."

Why wasn't he backing off? Shouldn't he be out of here by now, sorry he'd ever taken up with her?

If he was like most men, he'd already be gone. So what would she have to say to get him out of here before she did something stupid like look at him for a second too long—a second in which she might inspect the cracking sensation in her soul too closely and realize that there was a reason she was starting to hurt deep in her core?

Her heart was beating so hard that it'd affected her vision, muddling it, making time speed along so that she could barely keep up.

He seemed so hopeful, sitting there on her bed. Even as she was doing her best to let him know this could never, ever work out, he hadn't quit on her.

Surely he had to know that cutting this off now was the best thing they could do.

"I can't believe you don't know any better than this,"
she said softly. "I don't do love."

"That's bull."

He stood, and she turned away. *Please put on your
jeans,* she thought. *Please have enough sense to know
that this is over.*

But he was so hardheaded that he kept on talking.

"I don't know what flipped the switch and made me
admit how I feel for you," he said. "It could've been
watching you with Jack today. Tough, independent Laurel Redmond with a baby, a brightness in her eyes that
tells everyone who can see it that she's got a soft heart
after all. I saw you having your own child one day."

She was going to die if he said anything about it being
their child because right now she could see it, too, even
if she was trying like hell to banish the thought.

Still, she could feel a baby in her arms, smell his or
her skin as she held the child close.

And that child would have Sawyer's blue eyes...

She shook her head, as if to dislodge the image.
"Don't get all emotional on me. It's not fair."

"To do what? To get you to admit that there's a possibility that you do 'do love'?"

She rounded on him. "I don't have any feelings. Don't
you understand that?"

Silence bit down on the room.

Then he began to get into his jeans. Good. She'd gotten through to him. *Finally.*

So then why didn't it feel better? Why did it seem as
if she'd been gutted, emptied out until there was nothing left but...

Regret?

Apologies?

Or something else that she refused to confront?

She crossed her arms over her chest, waiting for him to be done, but after he pulled on his jeans, he didn't go for his shirt.

Her instinct told her that he was about to say something else—and it might just be this one thing that broke her down—so she launched a preemptive strike.

"All you're feeling is lust," she said. "Not love. It'll go away soon enough."

A slow burn seemed to consume him, and she hugged herself tighter, digging her nails into her arms, as if punishing herself.

"Speak for yourself," he said with such slow, strong conviction that she pressed her lips together.

Don't cry, she thought. *Survivors never cry.*

"What're you so afraid of, Laurel?"

His words were quieter now, and it took everything she had to hold herself together.

"I'm not afraid," she managed to say.

"You sure as hell are. I think you're afraid of being shattered again. You're afraid that I'm going to treat your heart like garbage and throw it away after I've used it. But I don't think you heard what I said—I love you, and I would never treat you as anything but a queen."

He was killing her bit by bit, one piece of her crumbling away, another following.

She had to collect herself before it was too late.

So she said the only thing she could think of that would make him stop.

"Steve told me he'd treat me like a queen, too, Fortune. And look where that went."

She didn't have to look at him to know he'd reached the boiling point…or that he would have a look on his face that would lance her straight through if she saw it.

Because she did feel for him. And it was going to finish her off if she didn't get out of here fast.

She rushed out the door, grabbing her keys from an ashtray near the exit, escaping, even though it was her own apartment.

As she jumped in her pickup and took off, tears flooded her eyes, and she swiped them away, pulling off the road and into a crowded parking lot because she couldn't drive anymore.

She'd left him before he could leave her, and she should've felt stronger for it. But she only felt weak, as if she'd given up something valuable and irreplaceable.

Something—no, *someone*—she really did love, even if it could never last.

Every day that passed from that point on felt like an empty box to Sawyer—a container that had once held a gift that'd been tossed aside without much care.

He felt more lost than ever, even more aimless than he had been when he'd first decided to strike out in a different direction in Red Rock.

And he knew exactly why he couldn't find himself anymore: it was because of Laurel, a woman who made him feel found for the very first time in his life.

She'd torn out his heart and spit it out last week, and he hadn't been the same since, walking around in a haze as New Fortunes Ranch was transformed into wedding hell for his brothers and their brides.

At the moment, he was standing at the front of his

Jag, leaning against his car and watching as the wedding planner ordered her crew around the large gazebo area. Tents would provide an extension of shade for the reception, and more latticework was being planted around the space; it would be covered by bougainvillea while temporary fountains splashed over fancy sculptures.

To the side of the gazebo, Shane, Asher and Wyatt were deep in conversation while looking at an iPad. Maybe they had downloaded plans on it. Sawyer didn't know.

It wasn't his wedding.

He'd been thinking about joining them today, helping out, but he just didn't have the stomach for it, and he got back into the car before they saw him.

Left behind again, Sawyer thought, starting the engine.

As he drove away, he peered into the rearview mirror. None of his brothers had even noticed he'd been there, but why would they when there was so much going on?

Sawyer wished he could talk to them about Laurel, but he didn't want to squash their happiness. He'd always been the guy who kept his issues to himself, anyway.

But this time, why did it feel as if it was too much to hide?

He drove and drove, not knowing where he was going until he got on the road to the airport.

Before he really knew what he was doing, he pulled over. He didn't want to go into the terminal; his hurt reminded him that he didn't want to see Laurel, even if he actually *did.* Besides, she'd been avoiding his phone calls—even the one telling her that he wanted her to come to his brothers' wedding—and he didn't want to force the issue and bother her at work.

No, he supposed it was the planes coming in and out that had drawn him, offering a measure of comfort.

He waited in his car, not feeling anything much, just listening to the muffled drone of the aircraft, watching them fly over and remembering the day Laurel had taken him flying.

It was almost as if it'd never happened.

He didn't know how long he sat there, but several cars passed him. Then one pulled over and parked in front of his own. It was a Tahoe, and Sawyer recognized the tall, dark-haired man in sunglasses who got out.

Tanner Redmond.

Since Sawyer had the top down on his convertible, he was exposed and he couldn't exactly burn rubber out of here. Crap.

"Just so you know," Tanner said as he approached the driver's side of the Jag, taking off his sunglasses, "Laurel's not in today."

Sawyer wasn't even going to ask if she was on a charter flight or at home.

"Don't worry," he said. "I'm not planning on going into your offices to see her."

"Great. Because I heard the two of you called it quits."

Tanner had that big-brother tone going on, but there was something in his eyes, too. It looked like sadness.

Sawyer said, "You know, I wasn't the one who broke things off. Did she tell you that?"

"No." A car passed, shooting over the road toward the airport entrance. "But I figured as much."

It was even more of a shock when Tanner gestured for Sawyer to get out of the car and join him outside.

They wandered away from the road, toward the unkempt vegetation. Tanner idly bent to pick a blade of the long grass, and it was clear that he didn't want to be here having this talk as much as Sawyer.

"She's been moping around," Tanner said, "looking just as put-out as you do."

If that was supposed to improve Sawyer's mood, it didn't. "I swear, I intended for her to be in a much better mood the last time we saw each other." He swallowed. "I told her I love her."

Tanner gave Sawyer the once-over. It was a pass-fail kind of look, and when Tanner glanced away, Sawyer had a feeling he'd passed.

"I wasn't sure about you at first," Tanner said.

"I didn't exactly come with the seal of approval on me. But Laurel's enough to make a man want to change for her. Or to make him realize his best qualities."

"You had an effect on her, too. That was plain obvious. She told me she was seeing you just for fun, but then I'd catch her at work, staring off into space with a dreamy smile, and I knew."

A whoosh of warmth came to life in Sawyer. "What did you know?"

"That she was crazy about you. And that's saying a lot with Laurel. She's been in self-imposed exile for a while, and she never puts herself out there when it comes to men." Tanner paused, then said, "You know about Steve Lucas, right?"

"As much as Laurel would tell me."

"I suspect that wasn't much."

"She said that he wormed his way into her heart, won her trust and then robbed her—and I'm not only talking about her bank account."

"That's just the surface of what happened." Tanner tossed away the grass. "You should've seen her afterward—she was a mess. The only thing that kept her sane was being in the Air Force reserves one weekend a month and a couple weeks during the summer. Even better, she traveled all over, as if she was trying to lose herself in foreign places. I loaned her the money, telling her she could pay me back anytime, and it says a lot that Laurel—the proudest of the proud—took it without arguing." Tanner shook his head. "I think the idea was to blend into each destination, forgetting about what'd happened in her own life."

Ouch. All this time, Sawyer had thought the travel had merely been wanderlust, but it'd been an attempt to heal.

Tanner said, "After my wedding, she settled here. Jordana was pregnant, and I think it was Jack that persuaded Laurel to stay. After he was born, she doted on him and was over at the house all the time. And it was good to see her giving her heart to someone again. She knew that Jack wasn't going to crush it."

"I saw how she acts with him. It's apparent how she feels."

Tanner grinned. "She keeps telling us that she'll be a single mom one day when she's ready."

"She told me that on the night I met her."

Both of them laughed. It was so Laurel.

But the laughter pained Sawyer, too, and it died inside of him.

Tanner noticed, and he narrowed his gaze, really reading Sawyer.

"Laurel acts like she doesn't care about much," he said. "But she does. She puts everything into caring, so when someone disappoints her, a part of her withers away. Our father set the standard for that, I'm afraid."

Sawyer met Tanner's gaze head-on. "I know about that, too, and all I ever wanted was to show her that she can count on me. What I feel for her is real."

"It'd better be real. Because I can't sit by and watch my sister go through another set of lost years because some guy was playing around with her."

"She just needs to give me a chance, Tanner. That's all I'm asking for."

"You'd better be one hundred percent sure about your intentions. If you dare hurt her…"

"I won't."

Tanner stared at him, then clipped out a nod. But he had a hint of a smile as he put his sunglasses back on.

"In that case, I'm going to tell you something—what Laurel needs is your patience. She's flipped out now, but if what I suspect about how she feels for you is true, then she'll come around. She's not a woman to be forced into anything. And she's no dummy. She'll come to her senses and know that you're not Steve Lucas or our father."

And if she didn't?

Sawyer didn't want to think about that.

He extended his hand, and Tanner shook it. But just as they were about to disconnect, Sawyer didn't let go, gripping Tanner even harder.

"I've never felt this way about anyone," he said. "Feelings like this…they come only once in a lifetime, and I want to spend the rest of mine with Laurel."

"You can tell her that yourself," Tanner said, slapping Sawyer on the back. "When the time is right."

As he left, taking off in his Tahoe toward the airport, Sawyer thanked his lucky stars that he'd been at the right place at the right time with Tanner.

And he was always going to be there for Laurel, too… if she would let him.

It was the day of the Fortune brothers' wedding, and Laurel couldn't hang around her apartment thinking about it anymore.

Since last week, she'd been trying not to let the sight of the kitchen remind her of Sawyer, of him standing at the sink. She was trying not to think of her bed as the place where he'd gotten to her, body and soul.

Today she didn't even have her job at the flight school to bring her out of her apartment, keep her busy, make her so tired that she could collapse on the sofa at the end of the day and sleep there, avoiding that bed.

So she decided to put on some running gear and drive to a park where there were jogging trails. Maybe she could exercise Sawyer out of her.

Or exorcise.

But as she ran, pushing herself until her lungs hurt, he still stuck with her.

That was when she realized why he wouldn't go away.

She'd fallen in love.

As she slowed down near a bend in the trail, she walked, her hands on her hips, her pulse kicking through her from the exercise as well as her pumping emotions.

She had no idea how to be in love. Steve had merely been a failed dress rehearsal, and how did a person recover from something like that?

How did you move on?

There was one person who would know, and Laurel had refrained from telling her about Sawyer, just as she had with most everyone.

But now she took her phone off its clip at her waist and brought up her mom's number.

As her phone rang, Laurel paced.

"Laurel!" her mother said when she answered.

She sounded so excited, and Laurel wished she could feel that way again, too. But Sawyer was the one who brought joy to her life, and she'd chased him away.

"Hey, Mom. You busy?"

"When it comes to you, never. You sound winded."

"I was taking a run."

"I'm just cooking up some samosas to put in the freezer."

Laurel could imagine her in her kitchen in Tulsa, making good on those cooking lessons she'd signed up for.

Mom added, "I won't have much time for complicated meals this coming month. I decided to take ballroom-dancing lessons."

Laurel smiled at the evidence of how her mom was going out, living, when she could've still been curled up and crying because of how her ex-husband had treated her.

"That's so great, Mom."

"I know." She paused. "Honey, is something wrong?"

From the tone of her voice, Laurel could tell that Mom already knew about Sawyer. Damn Tanner.

Mom said, "You sound just awful. I was going to call you, but Tanner reminded me that you would reach out when you needed to."

Was she really that much of a loner?

The extent of her self-appointed alienation hadn't hit her until now, after what she'd done to Sawyer…and herself.

"What did Tanner say?" Laurel couldn't even be mad at him for blabbing.

"Just that you met a man. Sawyer Fortune. And that you…liked him."

"Except it's not so much in the past tense." Laurel kicked at a stone on the dirt. "I'm an idiot. I had something good going on with him, but I wigged out when he wanted to get serious."

"Did you want to get serious?"

"I didn't think so. But now that he's gone…" Laurel leaned back her head. "Yes. I think I do."

"If you're only thinking about it, then I'd reassess your feelings, honey."

She was right. Mom was always right.

"Then I know I do, Mom," she said. Wetness was leaking out of the corners of her eyes, but she didn't bother drying the tears. It might feel good to cry. She hadn't allowed herself to really let loose with it yet.

She sat down on a flat rock as her mother spoke.

"Laurel, you're a strong woman, but is it the kind of strong that makes you happy? Or is it the kind of strong that's going to isolate you for the rest of your life?"

"I've got you, Parker, Tanner and Jordana and Jack."

And in the future, an adopted child, or one she could have on her own.

But that sounded so sad when she could be with someone, have a family with him.

Mom's voice soothed. "That's how I used to go about life after your father left. At first I pretended like he hadn't hurt me. I raised you kids and loved you and put all my energy into you and my jobs, but it wasn't enough, Laurel. And I wasted so much time lying to myself about it."

Now the tears were coming, and Laurel rested her elbow on her thigh and pressed her hand against her forehead. She'd become her mom, hadn't she? And she'd told herself for so long that she'd never have her heart broken like her mother had, that what Steve had done to her was temporary and she could live through it.

But how much time had she wasted with those lies?

"Laurel," Mom said, "I spent too much effort trying to recover from a man who couldn't have cared less about me, and if you're using your bad experience with Steve to make excuses about avoiding loving and living life to its fullest, stop now. Take it from me—it's not worth it."

She was nodding, even if her mother couldn't see her. And when she spoke, it even sounded as if she'd been crying. But why hide it anymore? She'd had enough of hiding what she really felt.

"I don't know what to do. I said some pretty bad things to Sawyer."

"And he believed them?"

"No." Her throat was so tight that she could barely swallow. "He kept insisting that he loves me and that I love him. He's been calling, too, trying to get me to reconsider." And asking her to come to his brothers' wedding, even if she'd told herself that she didn't want to see him.

"So let me get this straight—you've got a man who's so in love with you that he's willing to put his pride on the line to get you back, and you're sitting here telling me you have no idea what to do?"

A tremulous giggle welled up in Laurel's chest, and she gave in to it. Mom laughed with her.

It was silly, wasn't it?

Maybe the scariest part wasn't telling Sawyer that she'd been wrong and that she wanted more than anything to give them a try. The most terrifying part was the future, and what might happen if he changed his mind about how he felt.

Laurel shook her head and snuffled away her tears. "How funny is this—I've been up in MC-130 Talons on missions. I've been fired on by enemy forces. And *this* is what's scaring me."

Mom laughed with her. "You always were a different girl, Laurel."

Sawyer had thought that, too.

But had he had so much time away from her that he'd reconsider his feelings? Had she already pushed him away enough that he'd changed his mind about how much trouble she was?

Laurel fought off the too-familiar doubts before they devoured her.

"I've got to go, Mom."

"You bet you do."

With a determined gait, she sped back down the trail so she could get home and see what she had in her closet to wear to a wedding.

Chapter Twelve

The day of the triple wedding dawned bright and sunny, shining down outside the church on what seemed to be a crowd composed of every Fortune who'd ever lived in Red Rock, mingling, waiting to be seated.

Sawyer's former Atlanta cousins—Michael, Scott, Emily, Jordana, Blake and Wendy—were with their significant others and any children. Some of them acted as ushers, but they were all generally making sure everything was running smoothly. Even Frannie and Roberto Mendoza and their kids, plus Lily and William and JR and Isabella, were in attendance, as well as what seemed to be every other Mendoza in town.

The only person Sawyer didn't see was Laurel.

Back before he'd talked to Tanner, Sawyer had made it clear to her that she was welcome at the wedding, but he shouldn't have been surprised that she'd stayed away. Even though Tanner had recommended leaving her to come to her senses on her own, Sawyer was getting more and more impatient every day.

He blew out a breath and went inside the back door of the church, hardly feeling social enough to stand outside and chat with his relatives and the guests. Besides, the ushers were shepherding everyone inside now, and Sawyer needed to report back to his own duty.

As he walked into the grooms' dressing room, Shane, Asher and Wyatt turned to him, all of them dressed in matching tuxes that made them look sharp and suave.

A sense of pride and love swarmed Sawyer, and his own problems fell away—except for the fact that he wished he could be more than their best man.

That he could be waiting for his own bride to come down the aisle.

"Look at you monkeys in your suits," he said. It was better than being maudlin.

Shane couldn't stop grinning, but then again, the same went for Wyatt and Asher.

"Are things on track out there?" he asked.

"Chugging right along." Sawyer went up to Asher and adjusted his slightly crooked bow tie. "They should be summoning you victims out there soon enough."

None of them said anything for a few seconds. They just looked at each other, knowing that their lives would never be the same.

At least that was true for the grooms, Sawyer thought, a pit of emptiness widening inside him.

Just as Sawyer was about to crack another joke to make sure none of them started getting all mushy with each other, someone knocked on the door, and he went to answer it.

Saved, he thought, opening up to find his mother there, fairly glowing in a light-pink designer dress with a skirt that came to her knees, a scooped neckline and shawl collar. She looked ready to burst with smiles and weep at the same time as he let her in.

"Just checking on my boys," she said, heading straight for Asher. She fussed with the bow tie Sawyer had just adjusted.

She had an anxious energy, but it wasn't just about her sons getting hitched.

Their father had taken off a day or two earlier, honoring Shane's, Asher's and Wyatt's wishes that he not attend the wedding. Although Shane had made peace with Aunt Jeanne, encouraging Asher and Wyatt to take steps to do the same, they were still pissed at Dad.

Sawyer knew that this elephant in the room needed to be addressed, so he went for it.

"Dad isn't out there?"

"No," she said.

His brothers set their jaws, and Sawyer could tell that, even though they were angry with Dad, they had still been hoping he would ignore their tempers and come to the ceremony anyway.

Clara turned to Sawyer, her hands folded in front of her. But her knuckles were white.

"I wasn't going to say anything to any of you since I didn't want to cause a stink, but James told me he *would* be here." She glanced at the others. "He told me that, no matter how disgusted you were with him, he didn't want to miss such an important day in your lives."

"Nevertheless," Sawyer said, "he's MIA."

Their mother nodded, then raised her chin a notch.

"The cynical part of me is wondering if he was only placating me by saying he would be here and he never intended to be. Perhaps he didn't want to rock the boat with you boys and he thought it was best to stay away."

Really? Dad had to pull this, and on such a special day?

Sawyer had had enough, and he excused himself from the room, slipping out the back and getting out his phone.

He dialed his father's number, but all he got was voice mail.

"Dad," Sawyer said, "this is ridiculous. Call me back ASAP. There's no family fight in the world that should be keeping you away from your sons' wedding, even if you're standing in back of the church incognito, for God's sake."

He hung up. To think, he'd believed their father had turned some kind of corner, not only with him, but with the realization that family should always come first.

When he went back into the dressing room, his mother had left.

Wyatt shook his head. "She's trying to delay the ceremony now. In spite of what she said, I think she really believes that Dad's just late or something. She still has hope he'll come through."

"Doesn't she always?" Asher sighed. "I'll tolerate one delay, but no more than that. You know Dad—we could be here all day long. The man's so stubborn that I wouldn't be surprised if he *didn't* come."

Shane cursed, then cut himself off, no doubt realizing a church was no place for it.

All in all, the three of them seemed regretful that

things had turned out this way. But they'd been just as stubborn as Dad.

Sawyer checked his messages, but that didn't magically make his father call, and by the time he and his brothers were called out to the altar, they still hadn't heard any word from him.

But what could Sawyer do?

He could be the most supportive best man three brothers could have—that's what.

When he accompanied Shane, Asher and Wyatt to the altar, he gave them reassuring smiles. Proud smiles. And as he looked around the church at everyone attending, he tried not to think about someone else who was missing.

Laurel. Missing from the ceremony.

Missing from his life.

He attempted to concentrate on the fact that Uncle John and Aunt Virginia were here, and strangely, they were sitting on either side of Aunt Jeanne, who was wearing a yellow dress with her gray hair done up in a bun. It was anyone's guess what his uncle and aunt had said to each other when they'd been seated so closely, but Uncle John did have a pensive cast to his gaze.

Sawyer exchanged a glance with Shane, who'd invited Aunt Jeanne. At least they had this consolation prize—partial harmony in the Fortune family between John Michael and Jeanne Marie.

The processional music began, and Sawyer readied himself to say goodbye to his siblings' bachelor days.

But then…

Then the room lit up as the church door opened and one more person slipped inside, taking a seat in the back pew.

Laurel?

A little piece of Sawyer's heart chipped off at the sight of her in a flowered dress, her hair down. He couldn't see her expression, but he took it as a good sign that she'd come.

For him?

He wouldn't even start to hope.

But why else would she be here?

The bridal party began to walk down the aisle, and when his sister, Victoria, approached the altar, playing the part of bridesmaid, Sawyer smiled at her because she looked so pretty…and because Laurel was here.

But would he be smiling after he talked to her?

When the three brides appeared, Sawyer forced himself to concentrate on them, and his chest got tight. His brothers' futures, coming down the aisle, all resplendent in white dresses and holding bouquets of different flowers: pink calla lilies for Lia, ivory French tulips for Sarah-Jane and blue hydrangeas for Marnie. Shane, Wyatt and Asher couldn't take their eyes off them.

And Sawyer couldn't help but look at Laurel again after the brides came to the altar.

He couldn't imagine living another day without her, but right now, he had to turn around and be a part of the ceremony.

Still, he could feel her gaze on him the whole time.

Or was that just his imagination?

It didn't matter—everything was going by in a blur, in a stream of speed that was getting him closer and closer to the moment when he could go to Laurel.

Faintly, he heard the minister transitioning from the readings and sermon to the actual marriage.

"I now invite you to join hands and make your vows..." he started.

There was a shout outside the church, and the minister stopped talking.

When the doors opened and Dad came through them, towing a woman behind him, all Sawyer could hear was the sound of everyone turning around to gape.

James was smiling as he rushed down the aisle, bringing the mystery woman to the front of the church, where the father of the grooms was supposed to sit.

"Sorry for the interruption," he said, still beaming. That's when Sawyer—and everyone else—got a good look at the woman.

Jeanne Marie?

She had the same tall frame, the same gray hair swept up in a bun, the same...everything.

But Jeanne Marie was already present, and she was just as openmouthed as the rest of the church as she sat next to Clara and near John, who trained his wide eyes on this new mystery woman, then back to Aunt Jeanne.

Dad faced his sons and their brides at the altar. "I thought you all might agree—family is family, and I wasn't going to miss my sons' weddings. Sorry for the entrance, but we got here as soon as we could. I wanted to make sure that the *whole* family could be here!"

The church was buzzing, wedding or not. Sawyer could hear the whispers that echoed his own questions as he looked at the new woman who could've been not only Dad's twin, but Jeanne Marie's.

Shane stepped forward, off the altar. "Dad? What's going on?"

James Marshall Fortune glowed as he presented the

doppelgänger, who was blushing furiously. "I got word from my P.I. yesterday that he'd hit the mother lode. Jeanne Marie and I aren't twins. We're triplets!"

Next to Aunt Jeanne in the pew, Mom looked about ready to pass out. Uncle John was still staring at his new sister. Most everyone else in the church was gasping and whispering to each other in shock.

Even Shane, Wyatt and Asher had stunned expressions on their faces, along with their brides'.

Dad turned to the crowd. "May I introduce Josephine May Fortune. I wanted to get her here to see her nephews marry their beautiful brides, and it looks like we made it in the nick of time!"

Sawyer was still speechless. A triplet?

Asher held out his hands in a there's-a-lot-more-you-could-be-telling-us gesture. "Dad?"

James Marshall hugged his new sister to him. "I didn't want to reveal everything to you all until I was absolutely sure, but my P.I. had found some hints that there was another Fortune sibling out there somewhere. I had my suspicions, too, but it sounded…too odd. So I waited for confirmation and did more searching on my own."

Realization dawned on Sawyer as he recalled something Dad had said during the family meeting.

"That's right," he said. "You told us that there were two pink baby blankets that you found in Grandma's things. Pink, as in girls."

"You've got it, Sawyer." Dad gave him a respectful look that warmed Sawyer through and through, then continued.

"The evidence started to mount with the P.I., and when he tracked down Josephine, it turned out that my triplet ended up in a much different place than Jeanne Marie, who's lived in Horseback Hollow this whole time." He smiled at Josephine. "But that's a story for after the wedding. What do you say we get on with it?"

The crowd applauded, but then James waved it down as Josephine…no, Aunt Josephine…took her seat, leaning over to Jeanne Marie and clasping hands with her. But that wasn't enough for Aunt Jeanne—she sprang up and embraced her sister while Uncle John and Aunt Virginia scooted down the pew, allowing the sisters to sit next to each other.

Uncle John kept watching them. What was going through his mind?

After James was seated, he made a go-ahead motion. The grooms all shook their heads, then nodded to the minister.

In spite of everything, Shane, Wyatt, Asher and even Victoria seemed overjoyed that their father had arrived… and in such grand style.

The minister cleared his throat. "As I was saying…"

After one last curiosity-laden whisper from the audience, he went on to lead the exchange of vows, and when he asked, "Will you have this woman to be your wedded wife, to love her, comfort her…?" Sawyer took a risk.

He glanced to where Laurel was sitting.

He could see her among all the others, standing out from the masses, just as clear as a new day for him.

She held his gaze, half smiling, as if trying to keep tears at bay.

And when the minister got to the part about having and holding from this day forward, for better or worse, Sawyer couldn't help himself. It was a happy day, a day for miracles, after all, and he took the biggest chance of his life and mouthed "I do" to her.

Her smile only grew as she nodded and mouthed three words back to him.

"I do, too."

Fireworks went off inside Sawyer, and he didn't hear or see anything until the minister, with a flourish, ended with, "I now pronounce you husbands and wives!"

Sawyer had never heard applause like this, as the grooms kissed their brides and everyone stood up, already celebrating. And he felt the applause within himself, too, waiting for the moment when his brothers and sisters-in-law walked down the aisle with each other so he could follow them and go to the woman he loved.

The woman who loved him back.

He rushed down that aisle, wasting no time, deviating from the wedding party when he got to Laurel's pew.

She'd already stood and gone to the back of it, out of the way, anticipating his arrival, her hands fisted at her sides as if she didn't know what to expect.

But he didn't keep her waiting, sweeping her into his arms and twirling her around as she clung to him.

He was barely aware of everyone filing out of the church as he walked her over to the corner, his arms full of her, her hair raining over him, enveloping him in the clean Laurel scent he'd missed so much.

"I'm sorry for running off," she said in his ear, over the music and the chatter. Her tone was brimming with heartfelt sincerity that lifted him up higher than he'd ever gone before, even in a plane.

"*I'm* sorry for scaring you off," he said. "But I can't apologize for loving you."

"You shouldn't." She looked at him as he lowered her to the ground, keeping his arms around her. "Don't you ever apologize for that. I might have a funny way of showing it, but I love you, too, Sawyer."

And right there, as if they were at the altar, they came together, kissing, making their own vows.

His head was in the clouds, his body flooded with the warmth of being loved forever and always, from this day forward.

Even when the church was empty, they embraced, as if never wanting to let go.

But soon enough, she laughed, looking up at him.

"It's been quite a day," she said.

He got her meaning. Dad. Aunt Jeanne.

Josephine May.

"You should find out what's going on," she said.

"Only if you come with me."

He took her by the hand and she grasped it, no hesitations, no doubts.

Energized, he brought her out of the church, where William Fortune was lingering in the front along with most of the guests. The older man, who had refereed Sawyer's family at the Double Crown Ranch, didn't say a word, merely playing mediator again by pointing in the direction he no doubt knew Sawyer wanted to go.

To the rest of his family.

After waving a thanks to William, Sawyer found his clan—new wives and all—in the rear courtyard of the church, grouped together, the wedding photographer standing by, obviously having been ordered to wait until family business had been taken care of.

Everyone seemed to be waiting for Sawyer, as if

they'd known enough not to bother him and Laurel in the church. But they only seemed impatient, not angry. Maybe Shane, Asher and Wyatt had even needed the time to make amends with Dad while they were waiting.

Whatever the case, Mom stood on one side of Dad, grasping his arm and gazing adoringly at him, and Aunt Jeanne and Josephine were on the other side, holding hands. They didn't look any different at all, except for a regal aura that Josephine seemed to have, with her up-swept gray hair and expensive powder-blue suit.

Victoria noticed Sawyer and Laurel first, then every-one else turned to them, their gazes lighting up when they saw that they were an official couple.

"It's about time," Victoria said, and Sawyer didn't know if she meant that it was about time he arrived or it was about time he and Laurel got together.

Then Asher spoke up. ""I'm dying to hear the de-tails, Dad. Finally."

Sawyer squeezed Laurel's hand, then settled in for a good listen.

"So this is why I've been jetting here and there the past few months," Dad said, and Sawyer remembered how his children had cut him off from explaining more on the day of that explosive family meeting. "And, as I told you, all the clues came together to reveal this— Jeanne and Josephine. You'll never guess where I found our last piece of the puzzle, though." He rested a hand on Josephine's arm.

She smiled and touched her brother's fingers as he continued.

"Right in the lap of luxury."

Aunt Jeanne laughed and hugged Josephine to her.

"You can tell, can't you? Just look at these duds she's wearing."

Josephine had a dainty way of blushing, and when she spoke, she had a crisp accent. "I've been in England—"

Dad interrupted in his excitement. "And she was married to a member of British royalty! Can you believe that?"

Sawyer peered down at Laurel, who made an impressed face. God, his family. Did the fun ever end?

Still, he was curious about his new aunt. "Do we get to meet our esteemed uncle?"

A little of the happiness went out of Josephine's eyes. "I only wish it were possible. He's been deceased for years now." Then she smiled when Aunt Jeanne squeezed her. "However, he would have been equally gobsmacked to know that I was adopted."

"I wonder," Dad said, "what your husband would've thought of your new family, Josephine."

"As I am, he would have been uncertain as to what he should think of all you cowboys." While everyone laughed, she glanced at Jeanne Marie. "But it's even stranger—and more wonderful—to meet a woman who looks precisely like me."

The two of them embraced, and when James Marshall Fortune—the formerly steel-hearted magnate—wrapped his arms around his sisters and held them tight, everyone joined them in a huge hug.

Sawyer and Laurel were laughing and uniting with the group embrace, too, as he said over the din, "You can never have enough family!"

For once, everyone seemed inclined to agree.

When the group finally broke apart, Sawyer saw that

there'd been someone in the midst of the massive hug that he hadn't seen.

Uncle John was standing next to his new sisters, his hands on their shoulders as he looked at his brother.

"I can't believe it," he said, emotion weighing down his words. "But you three do share an uncanny family resemblance. You all look just as I remember our mother did."

As he broke off, Dad came forward to put a hand on *his* shoulder. It seemed to give Uncle John the strength to continue.

"We've lost so much time together over the years. I'm sorry, James, for ever doubting you. We've got a lot to catch up on."

As they all came together, the triplets and their older brother, Sawyer glanced at Laurel. She had a tear running down her cheek, as if their comments had spoken to her in a profound way.

Was she thinking about all the time *she'd* wasted being so defensive about love?

He slipped a finger under her chin, turning her face to his. And when she smiled at him, it wasn't the past he saw coloring her eyes.

It was the future—a bright, endless blue that he fell into as if it were a stretching summer sky.

"Do you mind joining such a crazy family?" he asked.

She laughed, holding on to him. "You know I've always wanted a family on my own terms, and I think I'm really going to love crazy…just as much as I love you."

As gaiety surrounded them, he kissed her again, for better or worse.

From this day forward.

Epilogue

Three months later, as autumn colored the trees outside the windows of Sawyer's bedroom, Laurel took a break from packing boxes to watch the wind blow a tumbleweed over the ground.

She used to feel that way—tossed around, lacking direction even if she had all the plans in the world. But without someone to love, there'd been nowhere she'd truly belonged.

Until now.

Glancing at the platinum cushion-cut diamond ring on her finger, she smiled so hard that she wasn't sure it would ever disappear from her face.

Who would've guessed that she'd be engaged one day? The woman who'd almost written off romance forever had been claimed by a man.

But not just any man.

Sawyer walked into the room, dodging all the open

boxes that had been stuffed with his clothing and other odds and ends. "I didn't know I had so much junk."

Neither had she, until she'd woken up and realized that she couldn't live without him. All *her* excess mental junk had been easy to get rid of after that.

"We'll sort through your stuff and deal with it," she said.

He came to her, putting his arms around her and tickling her tummy as she squealed and leaned her head to the side.

When he eased up, she asked, "So are you going to miss it here on the ranch?"

"We'll visit. Horseback Hollow isn't so far away that we won't be able to eat tapas at Red or visit Jack—or have your nephew visit *us*."

Laurel didn't stress out about not seeing Jack as often, even if she was in another place. Once the former Atlanta Fortunes had started to visit their new cousins and relatives in Horseback Hollow, they'd developed an interest in the quaint, charming town. Even Tanner had revealed that he'd been thinking of opening another flight school, and he'd asked Laurel to head it up, basing it just outside Horseback Hollow.

Always eager for an adventure, she'd said yes—but only if Sawyer agreed to come with her.

He'd been ecstatic about getting to know his extended family, and she shouldn't have doubted his sense of adventure, which matched hers in every way.

As he continued to hold her against him, she rested her head on his shoulder. "It's crazy to think that there was a little town, not all that far away, where a bunch of

Fortune relatives have been living. You guys just multiply everywhere, don't you?"

"We've always had a master plan to take over the world. Didn't you know?"

They laughed and he nuzzled her neck, talking into it.

"I hear Aunt Josephine is going to be visiting soon."

"That's Lady Josephine to you and me, mister."

"Yeah. I need to remember all that British title stuff. What'll you do with me if I create some sort of huge international incident with my ignorance?"

"Leave you in a stone-cold minute."

She turned to him, bringing him into a long kiss that said she was kidding, that she would never, ever leave him again.

The stars, the sun, the moon…it was all there in their kiss, whirling and swirling and making her dizzy every time she was with him.

She kept her forehead against his as they hugged.

"So how would you feel about getting married in Horseback Hollow?" she asked.

He didn't move for a second, but then he framed her face with his hands, looking into her eyes.

"Are you saying…?"

"That I'm ready?" She laughed, then nodded happily.

He kissed her again, this time with a joy so pure that it seemed to travel from him to her, heart to heart, soul to soul.

When he was done, he glanced around the room, at the boxes.

"What are you doing?" she asked.

He didn't answer until he went to a box, lifting out

two decorative vintage wooden shot glasses that he'd once kept on a minibar in this room. He gave one to her.

"A toast," he said before going to another box and pulling out a bottle of single-malt scotch and pouring it into their glasses.

He raised his, and it reminded her of the night they'd met, when they'd saluted being the lone survivors of the Red Rock Plague.

Even though they'd utterly failed in that, she raised her glass, too, because it'd been a victory after all.

"Here's to succumbing," she said.

He knew just what she meant, smiling and linking arms with her so they could both drink while entangled with each other.

"And," he said, "here's to new, unexpected beginnings to succumb to."

They threw back their scotch, and when he tossed away his glass into a box of blankets, she did the same, knowing just what he had in mind now.

But that was the beauty of them, she thought. Twin minds.

Twin hearts.

When he tugged a blanket out of a box and threw it over the floor, she was there before he was, pulling him to her and kissing him again.

She'd traveled the world and seen just about everything, but the lifelong trip she was about to take with Sawyer Fortune would be the grandest of them all.

* * * * *

When a dangerous storm hits Rust Creek Falls, Montana, local rancher Collin Traub rides to the rescue of stranded schoolteacher Willa Christensen. One night might just change their entire lives....

***

"Hey." It was his turn to bump her shoulder with his. "What are friends for?"

She looked up and into his eyes, all earnest and hopeful suddenly. "We are, aren't we? Friends, I mean."

He wanted to kiss her. But he knew that would be a very bad idea. "You want to be my friend, Willa?" His voice sounded a little rough, a little too hungry.

But she didn't look away. "I do, yes. Very much."

That pinch in his chest got even tighter. It was a good feeling, really. In a scary sort of way. "Well, all right, then. Friends." He offered his hand. It seemed the thing to do.

Her lower lip quivered a little as she took it. Her palm was smooth and cool in his. He never wanted to let go. "You better watch it," she warned. "I'll start thinking that you're a really nice guy."

"I'm not." He kept catching himself staring at that mouth of hers. It looked so soft. Wide. Full. He said, "I'm wild and undisciplined. I have an attitude and I'll never settle down. Ask anyone. Ask my own mother. She'll give you an earful."

"Are you trying to scare me, Collin Traub? Because it's not working."

He took his hand back. Safer that way. "Never say I didn't warn you."

She gave him a look from the corner of her eye. "I'm onto you. You're a good guy."

"See? Now I've got you fooled."

"No, you don't. And I'm glad that we're friends. Just be straight with me and we'll get along fine."

"I am being straight." Well, more or less. He didn't really want to be her friend. Or at least, not *only* her friend. But sometimes a man never got what he wanted. He understood that, always had.

Sweet Willa Christensen was not for the likes of him....

***

Enjoy a sneak peek at USA TODAY *bestselling author Christine Rimmer's new Harlequin® Special Edition® story,* MAROONED WITH THE MAVERICK, *the first book in* MONTANA MAVERICKS: RUST CREEK COWBOYS, *a brand-new six-book continuity launching in July 2013!*

REQUEST YOUR FREE BOOKS!
2 FREE NOVELS PLUS 2 FREE GIFTS!

H HARLEQUIN®

SPECIAL EDITION
Life, Love & Family

YES! Please send me 2 FREE Harlequin® Special Edition novels and my 2 FREE gifts (gifts are worth about $10). After receiving them, if I don't wish to receive any more books, I can return the shipping statement marked "cancel." If I don't cancel, I will receive 6 brand-new novels every month and be billed just $4.74 per book in the U.S. or $5.24 per book in Canada. That's a savings of at least 14% off the cover price! It's quite a bargain! Shipping and handling is just 50¢ per book in the U.S. and 75¢ per book in Canada.* I understand that accepting the 2 free books and gifts places me under no obligation to buy anything. I can always return a shipment and cancel at any time. Even if I never buy another book, the two free books and gifts are mine to keep forever.

235/335 HDN F45Y

Name	(PLEASE PRINT)	

Address		Apt. #

City	State/Prov.	Zip/Postal Code

Signature (if under 18, a parent or guardian must sign)

Mail to the **Harlequin® Reader Service:**
IN U.S.A.: P.O. Box 1867, Buffalo, NY 14240-1867
IN CANADA: P.O. Box 609, Fort Erie, Ontario L2A 5X3

Want to try two free books from another line?
Call 1-800-873-8635 or visit www.ReaderService.com.

* Terms and prices subject to change without notice. Prices do not include applicable taxes. Sales tax applicable in N.Y. Canadian residents will be charged applicable taxes. Offer not valid in Quebec. This offer is limited to one order per household. Not valid for current subscribers to Harlequin Special Edition books. All orders subject to credit approval. Credit or debit balances in a customer's account(s) may be offset by any other outstanding balance owed by or to the customer. Please allow 4 to 6 weeks for delivery. Offer available while quantities last.

Your Privacy—The Harlequin® Reader Service is committed to protecting your privacy. Our Privacy Policy is available online at www.ReaderService.com or upon request from the Harlequin Reader Service.

We make a portion of our mailing list available to reputable third parties that offer products we believe may interest you. If you prefer that we not exchange your name with third parties, or if you wish to clarify or modify your communication preferences, please visit us at www.ReaderService.com/consumerchoice or write to us at Harlequin Reader Service Preference Service, P.O. Box 9062, Buffalo, NY 14269. Include your complete name and address.

HSE13R

SADDLE UP AND READ 'EM!

This summer, get your fix of Western reads and pick up a cowboy from the HOME & FAMILY category in July!

BRANDED BY A CALLAHAN by Tina Leonard,
Callahan Cowboys
Harlequin American Romance

THE RANCHER'S HOMECOMING by Cathy McDavid,
Sweetheart, Nevada
Harlequin American Romance

MAROONED WITH THE MAVERICK by Christine Rimmer,
Montana Mavericks
Harlequin Special Edition

CELEBRATION'S BRIDE by Nancy Robards Thompson,
Celebrations, Inc.
Harlequin Special Edition

*Look for these great Western reads AND MORE,
available wherever books are sold or visit*
www.Harlequin.com/Westerns

HARLEQUIN

SPECIAL EDITION

Life, Love and Family

Be sure to check out the last book in this year's
Mercy Medical Montana miniseries by
award-winning author Teresa Southwick.

Architect Ellie Hart and building contractor
Alex McKnight have every intention of avoiding
personal entanglements while working together.
However, circumstances conspire to throw them
together and the result is a sizzling chemistry that
threatens to boil over!

*Look for Ellie and Alex's story
next month from Harlequin® Special Edition®
wherever books and ebooks are sold!*

HSE65753